INDECENT
ARRANGMENT

ALSO BY GENEVIEVE KINSMAN

ALIEN PRINCE

Alien Prince's Mate
Alien Prince's Crown
Alien Prince's Reign

INDECENT
ARRANGMENT

GENEVIEVE KINSMAN

Dragonfire Press Flame

Print ISBN: 979-8-89631-100-3

If you like the kind of stories that leave your imagination running wild, then this book is for you.

You might not like everything I write, and that's fine. We're consenting adults. But don't let one unlikeable story keep you from reading the others.

Chances are high you'll be missing out on something you really want. So, read them. Read them all. They're here for you.

For you.

GENEVIEVE KINSMAN

INDECENT
Arrangement

CHAPTER 1

The fluorescent lights of the hotel's employee parking lot flickered as I finally pushed through the back exit, my shoulders aching and my feet throbbing in shoes that had given up any pretense of support hours ago. I'd been on the clock since six that morning—fourteen hours of stripping beds, scrubbing toilets, and pretending I didn't notice the mess some guests left behind.

I slid into my beat-up Honda Civic and let my head fall back against the headrest, closing my eyes for just a moment. The steering wheel was cold beneath my palms, and I could see my breath clouding in the air. November in Oregon was unforgiving, especially when your car's heater had decided to join the long list of things in my life that had stopped working.

Two of my co-workers had quit yesterday—walked out mid-shift without even a backwards glance—leaving me alone to handle over fifty rooms. Fifty. My supervisor, Janet, had the audacity to tell me it was "character building" while she sat in her climate-controlled office doing God knows what. My back disagreed with her assessment.

I fumbled the key into the ignition and turned it, whispering a silent prayer to whatever deity handled broken-down vehicles. The engine coughed, sputtered, revved for a hopeful second, then died with a pathetic wheeze.

"No. No, no, no." I gripped the steering wheel hard enough that my knuckles went white. "Don't do this to me. Not tonight."

I couldn't afford a new car. I could barely afford the one I had. The last repair bill had eaten through most of my meager savings, and that was before Grandma's medication costs had gone up again. I was her only family close enough to help, and her fixed income barely covered her rent, let alone the prescriptions that kept her heart condition manageable.

I took a deep breath, counted to three, and tried again.

This time, the engine caught and held. The whole car shuddered like it was reconsidering its life choices, but it stayed running. I could have kissed the dashboard.

"That's my girl," I murmured, patting the cracked vinyl with something close to affection. I put the car in gear and pulled out of the lot, my mind already reaching toward the promise of warmth waiting at Jason's place.

My apartment's heating had gone out three days ago, and my landlord—a man who seemed to believe rental properties maintained themselves through positive thinking—kept promising "someone would look at it soon." In the meantime, the temperature inside my studio had dropped to match the outdoor chill. I'd woken up this morning able to see my breath, my fingers so stiff I could barely button my work shirt.

So Jason's place it was. We'd been together for over a year now, and I spent more nights at his house than my own anyway. He'd even given me a key last month, saying with that crooked smile of his that I "might as well make it official." I'd taken it as a sign we were moving forward, getting serious. Maybe even heading toward something permanent.

The drive to his neighborhood took twenty minutes, long enough for my mind to drift through tomorrow's to-do list: visit Grandma, pick up her prescriptions, call the landlord again, figure out how to cover next month's bills on the reduced hours Janet had "reluctantly" scheduled me for. The thoughts circled like vultures, but I pushed them away. Tonight I just wanted to curl up with Jason, maybe watch something mindless on TV, and forget about the disaster my life was becoming.

I turned onto his street and immediately noticed the unfamiliar car in his driveway.

A silver Mazda, newer and shinier than anything in our social circle could typically afford. I pulled up behind it and killed the engine, frowning. Jason hadn't mentioned having anyone over. Then again, he had friends I didn't know well—guys from the construction crew he worked with, occasionally bringing one or two around for beer and video games.

But as I walked up the driveway, I glanced through the Mazda's windows out of idle curiosity.

A makeup bag sat on the passenger seat. Beside it, a pink leather purse. A pair of women's sunglasses dangled from the rearview mirror. Several glossy shopping bags from boutique stores I couldn't afford to walk past, let alone shop in, were visible in the back seat.

My steps slowed.

The dread started as a small thing, a cold pebble dropping into my stomach. But it grew with each footfall on the concrete, spreading through my chest like ice water through my veins. My rational mind tried to intervene— maybe it was his sister's car, maybe a coworker needed a ride, maybe there was a perfectly innocent explanation—but some deeper, more primal part of me already knew.

I reached the front door and stood there, my keys clutched in my trembling hand. Through the window beside the door, I could see the living room was lit but empty. The TV was on, its blue glow washing over the furniture, but the volume was turned down so low it was essentially silent.

My fingers felt numb as I sorted through my keyring, looking for the one Jason had given me. The metal was cold, and my hand shook as I slid it into the lock.

I stood there with my hand on the doorknob, frozen.

Did I really want to know? If I walked away right now, I could convince myself there was an explanation. I could text Jason, wait for him to call me back with some reasonable story about who was visiting. I could preserve the illusion just a little longer.

But I'd never been good at lying to myself.

I turned the knob and pushed the door open.

The living room was exactly as I'd glimpsed it through the window—empty, but bearing the evidence of recent occupation. A few beer bottles sat sweating on the coffee table, condensation pooling on the wood Jason usually insisted I use a coaster on. The TV was tuned to some action movie, frozen mid-explosion.

And there, draped over the arm of the couch, was a shirt.

Pink. Definitely feminine, with thin straps and a plunging neckline. The kind of shirt you wore when you wanted to be noticed, wanted to be looked at. The kind of shirt I'd never been confident enough to pull off.

My throat tightened. I dropped my purse and keys on the small table by the door—muscle memory taking over while my conscious mind struggled to process what I was seeing—and turned toward the hallway that led to Jason's bedroom.

Each step down that hallway felt like walking through water. My heart was pounding so hard I could feel it in my throat, in my fingertips, in my temples where a headache was already beginning to bloom. I moved quietly without really knowing why. This was my boyfriend's house. I had a key. I had every right to be here.

And yet I crept forward like a thief.

As I got closer to the bedroom door, I heard voices. Low and muffled, but unmistakably there. A man's voice—Jason's voice—and a woman's, higher-pitched, breathless.

I pressed my ear against the door, my hand flat against the wood, and held my breath.

"Yes, just like that," the woman moaned, her voice thick with pleasure. "Harder."

The sound of flesh against flesh. A grunt from Jason. More moaning, building in intensity.

My vision blurred with tears, but I blinked them back furiously. I would not cry. Not yet. Not until I'd seen it with my own eyes, made it real, impossible to deny or explain away.

I grabbed the doorknob, twisted it, and shoved the door open so hard it slammed against the wall.

The overhead light was off, but the bedside lamp cast everything in a warm, golden glow that made the scene before me look almost romantic. Jason was on his knees on the bed, his hands gripping the hips of a woman on all fours in front of him. Her long dark hair cascaded down her back, and even in the middle of my heartbreak, I registered that she was beautiful—the kind of beautiful that came from expensive salons and gym memberships and a life without double shifts at cheap hotels.

Jason was thrusting into her, his face contorted with pleasure, and for a moment— just a horrible, suspended moment—neither of them noticed me.

I fumbled for the light switch and flipped it on.

The overhead light flooded the room with harsh white brightness. Jason's rhythm faltered. He thrust a few more times—whether from momentum or some kind of shocked autopilot, I couldn't say—before his head turned toward the door. Toward me.

His eyes went wide, his mouth falling open.

"What is it?" the woman asked, her voice annoyed at the interruption. She turned to look over her shoulder, following Jason's gaze, and when she saw me, her expression transformed into something I'd never forget.

She smiled.

Not a nervous smile, not an apologetic or embarrassed smile. A slow, satisfied smile, like a cat that had gotten into the cream and wanted everyone to know it. She pushed her hips back against Jason, grinding against him deliberately, and let out a little giggle.

"Madison," Jason said, his voice strangled. He pulled back, separating from her, and I caught a glimpse of his cock, glistening and still hard, and it broke something in me.

I couldn't breathe. Couldn't think. Could only feel the sharp, tearing pain in my chest where my heart was supposed to be.

I turned and ran.

"Madison, wait!" Jason shouted behind me, but his voice sounded distant, like it was coming from underwater.

My legs moved automatically, carrying me down the hallway while my mind spun in useless circles. This wasn't happening. This couldn't be happening. We were going to get married—he'd talked about it just last week, mentioned looking at rings, said he was saving up for something special.

I reached the front door and grabbed my purse with shaking hands, barely managing to shove my keys inside before flinging the door open.

"Madison!"

I glanced back—I don't know why, some masochistic impulse—and immediately wished I hadn't. Jason was in the hallway, completely naked, his body still flushed from exertion. All I could see was the image burned into my brain: him behind that woman, his hands on her hips, the expression on his face.

"I'm sorry!" he called out, and the sheer inadequacy of those words ignited something hot and furious in my chest.

I whirled around to face him. "You're sorry?" My voice came out as a shriek. "You're *sorry?!* Oh, well that makes everything so much better, doesn't it? You bastard! You fucking bastard!"

I was screaming now, loud enough that lights were starting to come on in neighboring houses, but I didn't care. Let them hear. Let everyone know what kind of person Jason really was.

"Madison, please, I'm sorry—" He was walking toward me now, his arms outstretched like he thought he could just hold me and make it all okay.

"Don't you dare!" I backed away, but he kept coming, and then his arms were around me, pulling me against his chest.

For one horrible, traitorous moment, it felt safe. Familiar. His scent, the warmth of his skin, the solid feeling of his body against mine—my body remembered a year of nights spent in those arms, even as my mind screamed at me to pull away.

"I'm so sorry," he whispered against my hair, over and over like a prayer. "I'm sorry, I'm so sorry, please—"

I almost believed him. Almost let myself sink into the apology, into the fantasy that we could somehow fix this.

Then I felt it. His cock, still hard, pressing against my thigh through my jeans.

The rage that flooded through me was clarifying, almost cleansing. I started to pull back, started to tell him exactly what I thought of his pathetic apology—

And then I saw her.

The woman was standing in the doorway, wrapped in Jason's sheet—*my* sheet, the one I'd slept under just last night—and she was grinning. Grinning like this was all some kind of joke, like my pain was entertaining.

"You bitch!" I screamed, wrenching myself out of Jason's arms. I started toward her, my hands already curling into fists. I wanted to wipe that smug smile off her face, wanted to make her hurt even a fraction as much as I was hurting.

Jason grabbed me from behind, his arms locking around my waist. "Madison, don't—"

"Don't touch me!" I thrashed against his grip, but he held firm. "Let go of me! Let GO!"

I managed to twist around to face him, and before I could think about it, before I could stop myself, my palm connected with his face in a slap that echoed through the quiet house.

Pain exploded through my hand, but I barely felt it. Jason's head snapped to the side, and when he looked back at me, there was a red handprint blooming on his cheek.

I shoved past him, stumbling toward my car. My vision was blurry with tears, my breath coming in ragged gasps that sounded almost like sobs.

"Madison, please, let me explain—" Jason's voice followed me.

"Fuck off!" I screamed without looking back. "Fuck off and die!"

Across the street, I could hear a door opening, voices murmuring. Someone shouted, "Dude, where are your clothes?" but I was too focused on getting to my car, on getting away from this nightmare.

My hands were shaking so badly I could barely get the key out of my purse. I dropped them once, had to bend down and scoop them off the cold pavement while tears streamed down my face and Jason kept calling my name.

Finally, finally, I got the door unlocked and threw myself into the driver's seat. I jammed the key into the ignition, and for once—for the first time in months—my piece-of-shit car started on the first try.

I peeled out of the driveway, my tires squealing against the asphalt, and I didn't look back. Not at Jason standing naked in his front yard, not at the woman who'd destroyed my life with a smile, not at the house where I'd imagined building a future.

The tears came in earnest now, hot and fast, blurring the road ahead. I swiped at my eyes with the back of my hand, trying to see clearly, but they just kept coming. Great, heaving sobs that made my whole body shake, that made it hard to breathe, that made me wonder how I was going to survive the next five minutes, let alone the rest of my life.

I drove without knowing where I was going, just needing to put distance between myself and the scene I'd left behind. The night was dark and cold around me, and I'd never felt more alone.

CHAPTER 2

I don't remember the drive home.

One moment I was fleeing Jason's neighborhood, tears streaming down my face, and the next I was sitting in my darkened living room, staring at the blank TV screen like it might offer me answers. The clock on the wall read 9:47 PM. Somehow, I'd made it back in one piece, though I had no memory of the turns I'd taken or the stoplights I must have passed through.

The apartment was freezing. I'd forgotten about the broken heater in the chaos of the last hour, but now the cold seeped into my bones, making me shiver. I pulled the ancient afghan from the back of the couch—a gift from Grandma years ago, the yarn faded and pilling—and wrapped it around my shoulders like armor.

My mind kept replaying the scene. The pink shirt on the couch. The sounds through the door. The way that woman had smiled at me, like my humiliation was a prize she'd won. And Jason—God, Jason—with his pathetic apologies and his arms around me and his cock still hard against my leg like I was supposed to just forgive him because he said the magic words.

I thought he was happy with me.

The thought came unbidden, and with it, a fresh wave of tears. I pressed the heels of my hands against my eyes, trying to stop them, but it was useless. My whole body shook with sobs I'd been holding back since I got in the car, great heaving things that tore out of my chest and left me gasping for air.

How long had it been going on? Was she the first? Had there been others, a whole parade of women I'd been too naive or too trusting to notice? Every late night at work, every guys' night out, every time he'd been too tired for sex—were those all lies?

A year. We'd been together for a whole year. I'd met his parents. He'd met Grandma. We'd talked about getting a place together, about maybe getting engaged by next summer. I'd been making plans, building a future in my head, and apparently I'd been the only one.

My phone buzzed against the glass coffee table, making me jump. The screen lit up with Jason's name and a photo of us from last month's hiking trip, both of us grinning at the camera, his arm around my shoulders. I watched it ring, my finger hovering over the answer button.

What would I even say to him? What could he possibly say to me that would make any of this better?

I let it go to voicemail. A minute later, it buzzed again. Then again. After the fifth call, I grabbed the phone and turned it off completely, tossing it back onto the table with more force than necessary.

The silence that followed was oppressive, broken only by the occasional groan of the old house settling and the distant sound of cars passing on the main road. I pulled the blanket tighter and tried to focus on something, anything, other than the image of Jason and that woman burned into my brain.

I must have sat there for at least an hour, numb and hollow, before my phone rang again.

Wait. That wasn't possible. I'd turned it off.

I stared at the device as it vibrated against the table, the screen glowing in the darkness. Right—I'd only thought about turning it off, but in my distracted state, I must not have actually done it. The caller ID showed Grandma's name, and guilt immediately washed over me. She was probably checking in, wondering if I was okay. She had that sixth sense about these things.

I pulled my hand out from under the warm blanket reluctantly and grabbed the phone, swiping to accept the call.

"Hello?" My voice came out rough, raw from crying.

"Hello, dear," came her fragile, familiar voice, and just hearing it made my throat tighten again. "I think I left my new prescription at your house when I stopped by this morning. Would you mind checking for me?"

Right. She'd come by before I left for work, bringing me some leftover casserole because she worried I didn't eat enough. We'd had coffee together at my tiny kitchen table, and she'd been telling me about the new medication her doctor had prescribed for her heart condition when I'd had to rush out the door to make it to my shift on time.

"Sure, Grandma." I forced myself up from the couch, my joints stiff from sitting in one position for so long. The blanket fell from my shoulders as I made my way into the kitchen, and the cold hit me like a physical thing. I wrapped my arms around myself and flipped on the light.

There, sitting on the counter right where she must have left it, was a white paper bag with the pharmacy logo. I picked it up and checked inside—two orange prescription bottles with her name printed neatly on the labels.

"Yeah, you did leave it here," I said, trying to keep my voice steady, trying to sound normal.

"Oh, thank goodness." I could hear the relief in her voice. "I thought maybe I'd lost them somewhere between your house and mine, and I already checked my car. Would you mind bringing them over? I need to take one before bed."

I glanced at the clock. It was past ten now, late for her to still be awake. She usually turned in by nine, like clockwork. The fact that she'd stayed up waiting for her medication made my chest ache with worry.

As much as I wanted to stay cocooned in my misery, wallowing in my self-pity and trying to process the disaster my life had become, I knew she really needed them. Her health had been precarious for months now—a series of small scares that had gradually escalated until her doctor insisted on the new medication. She was just starting to feel better, to have more energy, to sound more like herself again.

My comfort wasn't as important as that. It never had been, and it never would be.

Besides, maybe getting out of the house would help clear my head. At the very least, it would stop me from sitting in the dark replaying the same horrible scene over and over.

"Absolutely," I answered, mustering up something that might pass for enthusiasm. "Give me about fifteen minutes and I'll be there."

"Thank you, dear. You're such a good girl."
There was a pause, and then: "I'll be waiting
for you with some fresh cookies. Just pulled
them out of the oven."

Despite everything, I felt the ghost of a
smile tug at my lips. Of course she'd baked
cookies at ten o'clock at night. That was so
perfectly Grandma—always taking care of
everyone else, always making sure the people
she loved felt welcome and cherished.

"You didn't have to do that," I said.

"I know. But I wanted to. I had a feeling
you might need them tonight."

My eyes burned with fresh tears. She
knew. Somehow, she always knew.

"Thanks, Grandma," I whispered. "I'll see
you soon."

I ended the call and stood in the kitchen
for a moment, staring at the prescription bag
in my hand. Then I took a deep breath,
grabbed my shoes from where I'd kicked them
off by the door, and started getting ready.

The temperature had dropped even more
since I'd gotten home. I could feel the chill
radiating through the walls, could see my
breath misting faintly in the air. I pulled on

my heavy jacket—a thrift store find from last winter, the zipper slightly sticky and one pocket torn—and grabbed my keys from the hook beside the door.

Outside, the night was sharp and clear, the sky scattered with stars I never noticed when I was rushing to and from work. My breath came out in thick white clouds, and goosebumps immediately rose on my arms despite the jacket. If I didn't know any better, I would have sworn winter had arrived a month early. The forecast had said something about an unusual cold snap moving through the area, temperatures dropping into the low thirties.

I walked to my car and slid into the driver's seat, wincing as the cold vinyl bit through my jeans. I turned the key in the ignition.

The engine cranked. Sputtered. Wheezed. Died.

"No. Come on." I tried again, pumping the gas pedal the way my dad had taught me years ago, before he passed. "Please. Not now."

The car cranked again, the sound growing weaker, more pathetic. Nothing.

I tried a third time. A fourth. On the fifth attempt, there wasn't even a crank—just a sad clicking sound that meant the battery was giving up.

"Damn it!" I slammed my hand against the steering wheel, and the pain that shot through my palm—still tender from slapping Jason—only made my frustration worse. "Damn it, damn it, *damn it!*"

I sat there for a moment, forehead pressed against the steering wheel, trying not to scream. This day had been one disaster after another. The brutal shift at work. Coming home to a freezing apartment. Finding Jason in bed with another woman. And now my car, which had miraculously started when I needed to escape his house, had decided to strand me.

The universe clearly had it out for me.

But Grandma needed her medication, and I wasn't going to let her down. Not her. Not the one person in my life who'd never disappointed me, who'd always been there when I needed her.

I got out of the car and slammed the door with perhaps more force than necessary, then stomped around to the side of the house where I kept my bicycle. It was an old thing, a relic from my college days when I couldn't afford a parking pass and had to bike to campus. I hadn't ridden it in months—not since last spring, when I'd taken it on the nature trail that wound through the woods behind my property.

The bike was leaning against the house right where I'd left it, covered in a fine layer of dirt and probably spiderwebs I was grateful I couldn't see in the dark. I brushed off the seat and handlebars, then grabbed Grandma's prescription bag from where I'd set it on the porch and tucked it into the wicker basket attached to the front.

Now I just had to decide on a route.

The long way would take me through town, sticking to well-lit streets where I'd see the occasional car and maybe even a pedestrian or two. It would take thirty minutes at least, maybe closer to forty, and the thought of pedaling that far in the cold made my already-aching muscles protest.

The short way was the trail through the woods. Ten minutes, maybe fifteen. I'd taken it dozens of times in daylight, knew every turn and dip. But at night, with no streetlights and only the moon to see by, it would be treacherous.

And then there were the dogs.

For the past few weeks, people in the neighborhood had been talking about a pack of wild dogs running loose in the woods. Mrs. Coleman from two streets over claimed they'd gotten into her trash. Old Mr. Patterson swore he'd seen at least six of them slinking through the trees one evening, their eyes glowing in his flashlight beam. The local Facebook group had been buzzing with warnings to keep small pets inside after dark.

I'd never seen them myself, but then again, I'd been spending most nights at Jason's. The thought of his name sent a fresh stab of pain through my chest, and I shoved it away angrily.

I stared at the dark opening of the trail, barely visible in the ambient light from my porch. It would be stupid to take that route. Reckless, even.

But I was cold and tired and heartbroken, and the thought of adding an extra twenty minutes to this miserable errand was more than I could bear.

"Screw it," I muttered, climbing onto the bike. I'd be fast. Dogs probably wouldn't even notice me.

I pedaled around the back of the house and onto the trail, immediately swallowed by darkness. The moon provided just enough light to make out the general shape of the path ahead, but the trees on either side were solid black walls, their branches reaching overhead like grasping fingers.

My legs found their rhythm quickly, muscle memory taking over even though it had been months. The cold air burned my lungs with each breath, and my hands were already going numb where they gripped the handlebars. I should have worn gloves. Should have taken the long way. Should have done a lot of things differently today.

To distract myself from the encroaching darkness and the eerie silence of the woods, I let my mind wander. Inevitably, it wandered to the Wolf.

That's what everyone in town called him, though his actual name was Samson Lang. He owned the local bank—The Den, a name that played into his nickname so perfectly that no one could remember anymore which had come first. Was he the Wolf because of the bank, or was the bank called The Den because everyone already called him the Wolf?

My mother's ex-husband was not a kind man. Handsome, certainly—tall and broad-shouldered with silver-streaked dark hair and eyes that could freeze you in place. Business savvy, absolutely—he'd built The Den from a failing community credit union into the most profitable bank in the county. But kind? Merciful?

Not even close.

He was known around town for his ruthlessness when it came to debts. Miss a payment on your mortgage, and you'd get a polite call within twenty-four hours. Miss two, and you'd get a visit. Miss three, and you might as well start packing. He'd foreclosed on half a dozen properties in the past year alone, including the Hendersons' farm that had been in their family for three generations.

My mother had been married to him for five years—a mistake she'd realized within the first six months but had been too proud to admit for another four and a half years. She'd finally divorced him and run off to Hawaii with a man she'd met at some business conference, a wealthy tech entrepreneur who'd promised her everything Samson never had: warmth, affection, a life of leisure.

She'd tried to get the house in the divorce—her house, the one she'd lived in with Samson—but it turned out he'd purchased it in his name alone before they'd married. Even her expensive lawyers couldn't pry it from his grip.

Not that she needed it. She was living in a beachfront property in Maui now, posting photos on Facebook of sunsets and mai tais while I froze my ass off in Oregon, cleaning hotel toilets and getting cheated on by—

My front tire struck something hard.

I had barely a second to register the fallen branch stretched across the trail before the bike bucked violently beneath me. I flew over the handlebars, my body spinning through the air in what felt like slow motion, and then I hit the ground hard.

The impact knocked the wind out of me. I lay there gasping like a fish, my lungs refusing to work, panic rising as I struggled to breathe. Finally, mercifully, air rushed back in, and I sucked in great gulping breaths that tasted of dirt and dead leaves.

"Damn it," I wheezed, rolling onto my side. Every part of my body hurt. My palms were scraped raw where I'd tried to catch myself. My knees burned, and when I looked down, I could see dark stains spreading on my jeans—blood, probably, though it was too dark to tell for sure.

I struggled to my feet, testing my weight on each leg. Nothing felt broken, at least. Just bruised and battered, which seemed to be the theme of the day.

The bike lay on the other side of the branch, and I limped over to retrieve it. The front tire looked intact, though the handlebars were twisted at an odd angle. I straightened them as best I could, then lifted the bike over the branch and checked the basket.

Grandma's prescription bag was still there, thank God. At least something had gone right.

I was just about to climb back on the bike when I heard it: a rustling in the underbrush to my left.

I froze, my hand still on the handlebars, and peered into the darkness. At first, I couldn't see anything—just the solid black wall of the forest, impenetrable and menacing.

Then I saw the eyes.

Pairs of them, reflecting the faint moonlight, low to the ground. Moving toward me.

The shapes resolved into forms as they emerged from the shadows: dogs. Big ones, with matted fur and lean, hungry bodies. One, two, three... I counted at least five, maybe more behind them.

My heart kicked into overdrive.

I threw myself onto the bike and started pedaling, my scraped knees screaming in protest. Behind me, I heard the first bark—a sharp, aggressive sound that sent ice down my spine—and then the whole pack erupted into a chorus of snarling and howling.

It's one thing after another today!

My legs burned as I pumped the pedals as hard as I could, but I could hear them gaining on me, their paws thundering against the packed dirt of the trail. Closer. Closer. I didn't dare look back, but I could hear them right behind me now, close enough that I could hear their panting, could hear the snap of their jaws as they lunged for my back tire.

Up ahead, through the trees, I could see the place where the trail crossed over Harper Road. If I could just reach the road, maybe I could put some distance between us. The road sloped downhill from there, leading down toward town. Gravity would give me an advantage the dogs wouldn't have.

I was maybe twenty feet from the road when my tire hit something—a rock, a root, I couldn't tell—and the wheel jerked violently to the side.

For the second time in ten minutes, I went flying.

I hit the ground in an explosion of dirt and dried leaves, tumbling across the trail until I came to rest in a heap at the edge of the road. My entire body was one massive bruise. My palms were shredded. My knees felt like someone had taken sandpaper to them. When I tried to move, everything hurt.

But I could hear the dogs closing in, and fear overrode pain.

I crawled away from the ruined bike—one wheel bent at an impossible angle, the chain hanging loose—and forced myself to my feet. My right ankle protested, sending a sharp spike of pain up my leg, but I hobbled forward onto the road anyway.

Headlights appeared around the curve, bright and blinding.

A car was coming, moving fast. I quickened my pace despite the agony in my ankle, trying to reach the other side of the road before the vehicle reached me. The lights grew brighter, illuminating the scene like a stage: me, limping and bloody; the pack of dogs bursting from the trail behind me, their teeth bared.

Brakes screeched. The car came to a sudden, violent stop, the smell of burning rubber filling the air.

The noise frightened the dogs. They skidded to a halt at the edge of the road, their ears flattening against their skulls, and then they scattered back into the woods, disappearing into the darkness as quickly as they'd appeared.

Relief flooded through me, so intense it made me dizzy. I bent over, hands on my knees, and tried to catch my breath. I was safe. The dogs were gone. I was—

"Madison?"

The voice froze me in place.

I knew that voice. Deep and smooth, with just a hint of gravel at the edges. The kind of voice that could charm you into signing papers you'd regret or convince you that losing your family home was just good business.

I straightened slowly and turned to face the car. It was a sleek black Mercedes, expensive enough that it probably cost more than I'd make in five years. The driver's door was open, and standing beside it, looking at me with an expression somewhere between surprise and concern, was Samson Lang.

The Wolf.

My mother's ex-husband. The man who'd made her cry more times than I could count. The man whose reputation for ruthlessness preceded him into every room he entered.

And apparently, my rescuer.

"What are you doing out here?" he asked, his dark eyes sweeping over me, taking in my torn jeans, my scraped palms, my disheveled appearance. "Are you hurt?"

I opened my mouth to answer, but no words came out. After everything that had happened tonight—Jason, the car, the dogs—this was just too much. I stared at him, this man I'd spent years quietly resenting on my mother's behalf, and felt something in me crack.

I started to laugh. It came out harsh and slightly hysterical, and once I started, I couldn't stop.

My laughter cut off abruptly as the adrenaline that had been keeping me upright suddenly drained away. My knees buckled, and the world tilted sideways.

Strong hands caught me before I hit the ground. Samson's face swam into focus above me, his expression genuinely concerned now.

"Easy," he said quietly. "I've got you."

And then everything went dark.

CHAPTER 3

I came to slowly, awareness returning in fragments.

First, I registered the smell—leather and something expensive, cologne maybe, mixed with the new-car scent of luxury vehicle interiors. Then the sensation of movement, the smooth glide of a car in motion. Finally, the feeling of soft leather beneath me, cradling my battered body.

My eyes fluttered open.

I was in the passenger seat of the Mercedes, reclined slightly, a cashmere blanket tucked around me that definitely hadn't been there before I'd passed out. The dashboard glowed with soft blue lights, displaying more information than my entire car's instrument panel could dream of showing. Through the windshield, I could see the dark road passing by, illuminated by those painfully bright LED headlights.

"I didn't faint," I said, my voice coming out rougher than I'd intended.

Samson's eyes flicked to me briefly before returning to the road. "You collapsed. There's a distinction, apparently, though the end result looked the same from where I was standing."

I struggled to sit up, pushing the blanket away. "Where are we going? I need to get to my grandmother's house. She's waiting for her medication."

"I know. That's where we're headed."

I blinked at him, confused. "How do you—"

"You told me before you passed out. Well, before you started laughing hysterically and then passed out." He glanced at me again, and there was something in his expression I couldn't quite read. Concern? Amusement? "You had a rather eventful collapse."

Heat flooded my cheeks. Great. Just what I needed—to add "hysterical breakdown in front of my mother's terrifying ex-husband" to the list of today's humiliations.

"I didn't pass out," I insisted again, though even to my own ears it sounded weak. "I just... needed a moment."

"Of course." His tone was perfectly neutral, but I caught the hint of a smile at the corner of his mouth. "My apologies. You just 'needed a moment' and happened to lose consciousness while doing so."

I scowled and looked out the window, recognizing the landmarks now. We were only a few minutes from Grandma's house. I should probably thank him for the ride, but the words stuck in my throat. This was the man who'd made my mother miserable for five years, the man whose reputation for ruthlessness was legendary in Brookhaven.

And yet he'd stopped his car, caught me when I fell, and was now driving me exactly where I needed to go.

"Because leaving an injured woman on the side of the road at night with a pack of feral dogs nearby seemed like poor form, even for me." He said it matter-of-factly, without any hint of self-aggrandizement. "My reputation may precede me, Madison, but I'm not a monster."

The way he said my name sent an unexpected shiver down my spine. I told myself it was just the cold, the shock of everything that had happened, but some small traitorous part of my brain recognized it for what it was: awareness. The kind of awareness I had no business feeling toward this man, of all people.

I clutched Grandma's prescription bag tighter and focused on the road ahead.

We drove in silence for another minute before he spoke again. "Those dogs have been a problem for weeks. I've contacted the city animal control three times now, asked them to deal with the situation before someone gets seriously hurt." His hands tightened on the steering wheel, and I noticed for the first time how elegant they were—long fingers, neatly manicured nails, the kind of hands that signed contracts and foreclosure notices with equal efficiency. "They've gotten into the trash behind the Den several times. They're becoming more than just a nuisance."

The irony wasn't lost on me—someone nicknamed the Wolf complaining about actual canines invading his territory. I almost smiled despite myself.

"They nearly got me," I said quietly. "If you hadn't come along when you did..."

I didn't finish the sentence. Didn't want to imagine what might have happened if those dogs had actually caught me.

"But I did come along," he said simply. "So there's no point in dwelling on what-ifs."

We turned onto Grandma's road, and I felt a mixture of relief and something else—disappointment, maybe?—that the ride was almost over. The silence between us had shifted from awkward to something almost comfortable, and I found myself studying him from the corner of my eye.

He really was handsome. Devastatingly so, in that polished, powerful way that some men carried effortlessly. Even now, dressed in what I assumed were his work clothes—tailored slacks, a crisp white shirt with the sleeves rolled up to reveal strong forearms, no tie—he looked like he'd stepped out of a magazine spread. His short black hair was perfectly styled, his jaw sharp enough to cut glass, his brown eyes intense and intelligent.

My mother's new boyfriend might have more money, but Samson had something money couldn't buy: presence. The kind of raw charisma and authority that made people sit up and pay attention when he walked into a room.

An entirely inappropriate thought flitted through my mind—something involving those elegant hands and that authoritative voice in a context that had nothing to do with banking—and I shoved it away violently. What the hell was wrong with me? This was my mother's ex-husband. A man at least twenty years older than me. The person responsible for countless foreclosures and financial ruin in Brookhaven.

And I'd just caught my boyfriend cheating on me approximately two hours ago.

Clearly, I was having some kind of breakdown.

"Here," I said abruptly as we approached Grandma's driveway, eager to escape both the car and my own traitorous thoughts. "This is it."

He pulled into the dirt driveway, his expensive car looking absurdly out of place among the pink flamingos and garden gnomes that populated Grandma's yard. The headlights swept across the eclectic collection of lawn ornaments, and I saw his eyebrows rise slightly.

"Your grandmother has... distinctive taste in décor," he said carefully.

"She likes what she likes," I replied, a note of defensiveness creeping into my voice. "Not everyone needs to have perfectly manicured lawns and tasteful landscaping."

"I wasn't criticizing." He put the car in park and turned to face me fully for the first time since I'd regained consciousness. "I find it refreshing, actually. Most people are so concerned with what the neighbors will think that they forget to express themselves."

That surprised me enough that I met his gaze directly. His eyes were darker than I'd remembered, almost black in the dim light of the car's interior, and there was an intensity to his stare that made my breath catch.

"Well," I said, fumbling with the door handle in my haste to escape that penetrating gaze. "Thanks for the ride."

He smiled, and it transformed his face entirely—softening the harsh angles, reaching his eyes in a way that made him look younger, less intimidating. Almost approachable.

I heard him chuckle softly behind me as I shut the door, the sound doing absolutely nothing to calm my racing heart. The window rolled down smoothly.

"Take care of those injuries," he called out. "And Madison? Lock your doors at night. Those dogs are still out there."

I nodded mutely and watched as he backed out of the driveway. The Mercedes disappeared down the dark road, its taillights fading into the distance, and I was left standing in Grandma's yard clutching her medication and trying to process what had just happened.

A low hiss brought me back to reality.

I jumped and looked toward the porch, where a large tabby cat was glaring at me from beneath the rocking chair, its eyes reflecting the porch light like tiny green coins.

"Yeah, well, screw you too," I muttered, then climbed the steps and knocked on the door.

"Come in!" Grandma's voice called from inside, warm and welcoming as always.

I opened the door and stepped into another world entirely.

The house smelled like heaven—warm chocolate and butter and something else, maybe cinnamon?—and the aroma made my mouth water instantly. The interior was as eclectic as the yard, every surface covered with knickknacks and framed photos and little treasures Grandma had collected over her seventy-three years. Doilies on every table, afghans on every chair, a lifetime of memories displayed with pride.

It was cluttered and chaotic and absolutely perfect.

Grandma was sitting in her favorite chair by the ancient gas stove, her arthritic hands moving with surprising speed as she worked on what looked like a new blanket. She'd been knitting for as long as I could remember, creating a constant stream of afghans and scarves and mittens that she distributed to anyone who'd take them. Half the town probably had one of her creations tucked away somewhere.

She looked up when I entered, her weathered face breaking into a smile that immediately turned to concern when she saw my condition.

"Good Lord, child!" She set her knitting needles aside and stood up slowly, her movements stiff from sitting too long. "You look like you got into a fight with a badger and lost. What on earth happened?"

I held up the prescription bag like a trophy. "You wouldn't believe what I went through to get here."

She came over and pulled me into a hug, her small frame surprisingly strong despite her age. She smelled like cookies and lavender soap, the scent of home and safety and unconditional love. I felt tears prick at my eyes and blinked them back furiously.

Not now. I would not break down again. Not here.

When she released me, I looked down at myself and grimaced. My jeans were torn at both knees, the denim stiff with dried blood and fresh stains still spreading slowly. My jacket was covered in dirt and leaves. My hands were scraped raw, starting to swell now that the adrenaline was wearing off.

"I'll spare you the details," I said, trying for a lightness I didn't feel. "Can I use your bathroom to clean up? I promise I'll tell you everything after I don't look like I went ten rounds with a gravel road."

"You'd better." She shooed me down the hallway, but not before checking the oven with a practiced eye and adjusting the temperature. "And don't get blood all over my clean tiles. I just mopped yesterday."

The bathroom was quintessential Grandma—floral wallpaper, a collection of porcelain birds on a shelf above the toilet, handmade cross-stitch samplers with inspirational sayings framed on the walls. I locked the door and leaned against it for a moment, finally allowing myself to just breathe.

What a day. What an absolutely catastrophic, soul-crushing, nightmare of a day.

I caught my reflection in the mirror and winced. My hair was a tangled mess, full of leaves and twigs. My mascara had smeared, giving me a deranged raccoon appearance.

There was a smudge of dirt across my forehead. I looked like I'd been through a war.

Felt like it, too.

I turned on the tap and let the water run until it was warm, then began the painful process of cleaning myself up. My hands went first—I held them under the stream and watched the water turn pink, then brown as the dirt washed away. There was a small pebble embedded in my right palm, and I had to dig it out with my fingernails, biting back a curse as fresh blood welled up.

Grandma kept a well-stocked first aid kit under the sink—of course she did—and I found the peroxide and gauze easily. I poured the peroxide over my palms and watched it bubble and fizz, the sensation stinging but somehow satisfying. Evidence that it was working, killing bacteria, preventing infection.

Next came my knees. I had to strip off my jeans entirely, and the fabric stuck to the wounds where blood had dried. Fresh pain shot through me as I peeled it away, and I had to pause, breathing through my nose, waiting for the worst of it to pass.

The scrapes were worse than I'd thought—deep gouges that would definitely scar, surrounded by ugly purple bruising already starting to bloom. I cleaned them as gently as I could, using washcloths from Grandma's neatly folded stack and trying not to get water everywhere.

More peroxide. More bubbling. More stinging.

I wrapped my knees in gauze as best I could, then did the same with my hands, the white bandages stark against my skin. I cleaned my jeans in the sink, scrubbing at the blood and dirt until my hands ached, then put them back on while they were still damp. Not ideal, but better than walking around in my underwear.

By the time I emerged from the bathroom, I looked marginally more human and significantly less like a crime scene victim.

Grandma was back in her chair, but she'd set out a plate of chocolate chip cookies on the kitchen table along with a tall glass of milk. The cookies were still warm—I could see the chocolate chips glistening, half-melted—and my stomach growled loudly enough that Grandma chuckled.

"When's the last time you ate?" she asked.

I had to think about it. Breakfast had been a granola bar eaten standing up while I brushed my teeth. Lunch had been... had there been lunch? I couldn't remember. The hotel didn't give us real breaks, just fifteen minutes here and there to shove food in our faces before getting back to work.

"This morning," I admitted, sinking into the chair and reaching for a cookie. "Maybe."

"Madison Ruth Carter," Grandma said, using my full name in that way that meant I was in trouble. "You need to take better care of yourself. You're working yourself to death at that hotel."

The cookie melted on my tongue, rich and sweet and perfect, and I closed my eyes in bliss. If there was one thing I wanted to learn from Grandma, it was this—how to bake things that tasted like love and comfort and home.

"I know," I said around the cookie. "But I need the money. Especially now that—"

I cut myself off, but it was too late. Grandma's sharp eyes had caught the hitch in my voice.

"Especially now that what?" she asked gently.

I took a long drink of milk, buying time, trying to figure out how to explain. But the words wouldn't come. Every time I tried to form them, I saw Jason and that woman, heard her moan, felt the gut-punch of betrayal all over again.

"Nothing," I said finally. "Just... bills. You know how it is."

Grandma studied me for a long moment, and I knew she didn't believe me. She'd always been able to see right through me, ever since I was a little girl. But she also knew when to push and when to let things lie.

"Well," she said, returning to her knitting. "You eat those cookies and drink that milk, and when you're ready to talk about what's really bothering you, I'll be here."

I nodded gratefully and reached for another cookie, watching her hands work the needles with practiced ease. The steady click-

click-click was soothing, rhythmic, a counterpoint to the chaos in my head.

It was then that I noticed the envelope on the table.

It was half-hidden under a magazine, but the logo was unmistakable: the Den, rendered in sharp black letters with a stylized wolf head incorporated into the design. Across the front, in bold red letters that seemed to scream off the white paper, was stamped a single word: IMPORTANT.

The envelope had been opened, the flap torn roughly like Grandma had been in a hurry—or upset—when she'd received it.

Dread settled in my stomach like a stone.

"Grandma?" I set down my cookie and reached for the envelope. "What's this?"

"Oh, that." She didn't look up from her knitting, but her hands faltered slightly, missing a stitch. "Just some paperwork from the bank. Nothing to worry about."

But her tone said otherwise. And the fact that she wouldn't meet my eyes said even more.

I pulled the letter out and unfolded it, my eyes scanning the formal business language, the official letterhead, the—

"You're being evicted?"

CHAPTER 4

"That bastard."

I said it out loud for what must have been the hundredth time, staring at the ceiling of Grandma's spare bedroom while moonlight painted silver patterns across the faded wallpaper. The house had gone quiet an hour ago, Grandma finally retiring after I'd insisted—repeatedly—that I was fine, that she should get some rest, that she needed to take her medication and go to bed.

But I wasn't fine. Not even close.

I was furious. The kind of bone-deep, righteous anger that made my hands shake and my jaw ache from clenching my teeth. And underneath that anger, threading through it like a poison, was something else. Something that felt uncomfortably like betrayal.

Which was ridiculous. Samson didn't owe me anything. He certainly didn't owe my mother anything—she'd divorced him and run off to Hawaii without a backwards glance. But this? Evicting an elderly woman from her own home? A woman who'd lived here for fifty years, who'd raised her children in these rooms, who'd buried her husband and still managed to make this house a place of warmth and love?

It was inexcusable.

I rolled onto my side, pulling the quilt—one of Grandma's creations, of course—up to my chin. The room was cold despite the space heater she'd insisted on setting up, and my scraped knees throbbed with a dull, persistent ache that matched the rhythm of my pulse.

The eviction letter had been brutally straightforward. Three months behind on mortgage payments. Final notice. Foreclosure proceedings would begin in thirty days unless the full amount—plus late fees and interest—was paid in full. The total came to just over four thousand dollars.

Four thousand dollars. It might as well have been four million.

Grandma had explained it all in her calm, matter-of-fact way that somehow made it worse. Her social security had been reduced due to some bureaucratic recalculation. She'd thought it was temporary, thought it would be fixed, so she'd used her meager savings to cover the shortfall. But months had passed, and the "temporary" reduction had become permanent, and now her savings were gone and she was drowning in debt she had no way to pay.

"I didn't want to worry you," she'd said, her weathered hands folded in her lap. "You have enough on your plate, dear. I thought I could handle it."

But she couldn't. And now the Wolf was circling, ready to take everything she had left.

Had he known? When he'd picked me up, driven me here, looked at me with those intense dark eyes—had he known he was foreclosing on my grandmother's house?

Of course he had. He knew everything that happened at his bank. That's what made him the Wolf—he was always three steps ahead, always in control, always aware of every piece on the chessboard.

Oh, I was going to the Den all right. First thing in the morning. And I was going to give Samson a piece of my mind that would make his ears ring for a week.

I played out the conversation in my head, rehearsing it like a script. I'd march into his office—no, into the bank lobby, make it public so he couldn't just dismiss me—and I'd tell him exactly what I thought of men who preyed on the vulnerable. Who used their power to crush people who couldn't fight back. Who smiled and offered rides and pretended to be decent while signing foreclosure notices.

In my imagination, I was eloquent. Devastating. My words cut through his composure like a knife through butter, and by the end of my speech, the entire bank would be staring at him, seeing him for what he really was. He'd realize the error of his ways, forgive the debt, let Grandma stay in her home.

It was a nice fantasy.

But even as I rehearsed my righteous anger, a small, traitorous voice in the back of my mind whispered: *He's a businessman. He forecloses on properties. That's what banks do. It's not personal.*

I shoved the thought away violently. I didn't care if it was business. This was

Grandma. This was her *home*. And I'd be damned if I'd let him take it without a fight.

Sleep came eventually, dragging me under despite the anger still simmering in my chest. My dreams were fragmented and strange—feral dogs with glowing eyes chasing me through dark woods, their barking echoing off the trees. And then the dogs transformed, became a single massive wolf with silver-streaked fur and eyes that looked almost human. Almost familiar.

The wolf didn't chase me. Instead, it stood between me and the pack, protecting me, and when it turned to look at me, I saw Samson Lang's face reflected in its eyes.

I woke with a start, my heart pounding, the dream already fading into nonsense. Gray dawn light filtered through the curtains, and I could smell coffee brewing downstairs. Grandma was already up, of course. The woman probably hadn't slept past six in the morning in her entire life.

My anger returned with consciousness, burning away the last wisps of the dream. Today. I'd confront him today.

I found Grandma in the kitchen. Eggs sizzled in a cast-iron skillet. Toast popped up from the ancient toaster. The coffee pot gurgled its final gasps.

"Good morning, dear," she said brightly, as if yesterday's revelation hadn't happened. As if she wasn't facing eviction in thirty days. "I hope you slept well. How are your knees feeling?"

"They're fine," I lied, sliding into a chair at the kitchen table. In truth, they hurt like hell, stiff and swollen beneath the bandages. "Grandma, about the eviction—"

"We'll figure something out," she said firmly, setting a plate of eggs and toast in front of me. "We always do. Now eat. You're too thin."

I wasn't hungry—my stomach was a knot of anxiety and rage—but I ate anyway because refusing would hurt her feelings, and she had enough to worry about without adding my stubbornness to the list.

The eggs were perfect. The toast was buttered exactly how I liked it. And with each bite, my resolve hardened. I was going to fix this. Somehow.

After breakfast, I insisted on doing the dishes while Grandma settled into her chair with her knitting. Then I kissed her cheek, promised I'd call her later, and started the walk home.

The morning was cold and crisp, frost still clinging to the grass in shadowed patches. I took the same route as the night before, and in daylight, it looked completely different—less ominous, almost peaceful. The trail through the woods was dappled with sunlight, and I found my ruined bicycle exactly where I'd left it, the front wheel bent at an impossible angle.

I grabbed the handlebars and started pushing it, the scraping sound of the damaged wheel against the ground a rhythmic accompaniment to my thoughts. By the time I reached my house, I was covered in sweat despite the cold, my breath coming in visible puffs.

Inside, I took a quick shower, wincing as the hot water hit my scraped knees and palms. I changed the bandages carefully, noting with grim satisfaction that the wounds looked clean, no signs of infection. Then I dressed in the nicest clothes I owned—dark jeans without holes, a burgundy sweater that didn't have any stains, my good boots—and pulled my hair back into a neat ponytail.

If I was going to confront the Wolf in his den, I'd do it looking as put-together as possible.

My car, in a rare moment of cooperation, started on the first try. I took it as a sign.

The entire drive to the bank, I rehearsed my speech. Refined it. Perfected it. By the time I pulled into the parking lot of the Den, I had every word memorized, every emphasis planned, every pause calculated for maximum impact.

The bank was housed in a building that had once been a historic hotel—three stories of red brick and large windows, recently renovated with gleaming glass doors and a sign that probably cost more than my annual salary. It sat on Main Street like a predator among prey, watching over the small shops and restaurants that surrounded it.

I got out of my car, slammed the door with perhaps more force than necessary, and marched up the steps.

The lobby was different than I remembered.

I'd been inside the Den a few times when Mom was married to Samson—awkward visits where I'd sat in the waiting area while she met with him about joint accounts or investment portfolios or whatever it was that married couples who actually had money discussed. But that had been years ago, and apparently he'd completely redecorated since then.

The space was sleek and modern now, all clean lines and expensive materials. Black leather chairs—the kind that probably cost more than my car—were arranged in intimate clusters around matching tables. Soft recessed lighting created pools of warm illumination. The walls were painted a deep charcoal gray that should have been oppressive but somehow made the space feel sophisticated instead.

And it was busy. Nearly every table was occupied by people in business casual attire, speaking in low, professional tones with bank representatives. The conversations created a soft ambiance, a murmur of financial transactions and investment strategies and loan applications.

What struck me most, though, was the staff.

They all wore the same uniform—black slacks or skirts, crisp white shirts, burgundy ties or scarves that matched the bank's branding. And they were all, without exception, attractive. Young, polished, with perfect smiles and impeccable grooming. It was like walking into a carefully curated catalog of beautiful people who happened to work in finance.

The Wolf clearly believed in presentation. Everything about this place was designed to project success, stability, trustworthiness. Even the people were part of the aesthetic.

A man who looked about my age—late twenties, with dark hair styled with just enough product to look effortless, a jaw that could have been sculpted by Michelangelo—approached me with a smile that probably made most women weak in the knees.

"Good morning," he said smoothly. "Welcome to the Den. Is there anything I can help you with today?"

All my rehearsed eloquence evaporated in the face of actually being here, actually doing this.

"I'd like to speak with the Wolf," I blurted out.

The words hung in the air between us. The man's professional smile didn't waver, but I saw something flicker in his eyes—surprise, maybe, or judgment. My face burned with embarrassment.

"I mean—sorry, I meant Samson. Mr. Lang. I'd like to speak with Mr. Lang, please."

God, I was already screwing this up.

The man's smile became slightly more fixed, more forced. "Of course. Do you have an appointment with Mr. Lang?"

"No," I admitted.

"I see." He pulled out a tablet and tapped on the screen. "I apologize, but Mr. Lang's schedule is quite full today. He has back-to-back meetings until five. However, I'd be happy to schedule an appointment for you. Let me check his availability..."

More tapping. More professional smiling. I could feel my carefully constructed plan crumbling.

"The next opening is in two weeks. The twenty-third. Would that work for you?"

Two weeks. In two weeks, Grandma would be that much closer to losing her home. In two weeks, the late fees would be even higher. In two weeks, it might be too late to fix this.

"No," I said firmly, surprising myself with the conviction in my voice. "Two weeks isn't going to work for me. I need to see him today. Now would be good, actually."

The man's composure cracked slightly. His smile became strained at the edges, and he glanced around as if looking for backup. Clearly, he wasn't used to customers who didn't accept his smooth deflections.

"I understand your urgency," he said carefully, "but I'm afraid Mr. Lang's schedule simply doesn't—"

"You can tell him his stepdaughter is here to see him."

The words came out before I could think better of them. Technically, it wasn't even true—Samson and my mother had been divorced for years, and I'd never thought of him as a stepfather. But it was close enough to the truth, and more importantly, it had the desired effect.

The man froze mid-sentence. His professional mask slipped entirely for a split second, and I saw genuine fear flash across his perfect features. His eyes widened slightly as they traveled from my face down to my clothes and back up again, as if he couldn't quite reconcile my casual appearance with the idea that I might be connected to his intimidating boss.

I could practically see the calculation happening behind his eyes: *Is she telling the truth? What if she is? What will Mr. Lang do to me if I turn away someone he knows and she complains? Is it worth the risk?*

"Of course," he said quickly, his demeanor changing entirely. "I'm so sorry, I didn't realize—Mr. Lang didn't mention he was expecting you today."

"That's because he isn't," I replied, allowing myself a small, grim smile. "This is what you might call an unexpected visit."

The man swallowed hard and gestured toward one of the empty tables. "If you wouldn't mind having a seat, I'll let him know you're here right away."

"Thanks," I said, settling into one of the ridiculously comfortable leather chairs.

He practically sprinted to the door marked "Employees Only" at the back of the lobby, disappearing through it like his life depended on speed. I smirked despite my anger. The employees here might look like models, but apparently they were terrified of their boss. Not surprising, given the Wolf's reputation.

I sat there, trying to look calm and collected while my heart hammered against my ribs. Around me, the quiet conversations continued, people discussing interest rates and mortgage terms and retirement accounts like their world wasn't falling apart. Like some of them weren't sitting here because they were desperate, drowning in debt, hoping the Wolf would throw them a lifeline instead of going for their throats.

A few minutes later—though it felt like an hour—the employee door opened again. The young man emerged first, walking quickly back to his station, relief evident on his face. He'd delivered the message and survived.

And then Samson stepped out.

The entire lobby went silent.

sentence. People looked up from their papers. Even the soft ambient music seemed to fade into the background.

Samson commanded attention without saying a word. He was dressed in a charcoal suit that probably cost more than three months of my rent, tailored so perfectly it might have been painted on. His white shirt was crisp and pristine, his burgundy tie—matching the bank's colors, of course—was knotted with precision. His dark hair was perfectly styled, his jaw freshly shaved, and when he moved, it was with the kind of fluid confidence that came from knowing he owned every inch of this space.

His shoes—expensive Italian leather, I was sure—clicked against the polished marble floor as he crossed the lobby, each step echoing in the silence. Everyone watched him. And he ignored them all, his dark eyes fixed on me with an intensity that made my breath catch.

"Madison," he said, and just the way he said my name—smooth, warm, with the hint of a smile in his voice—made me falter.

I stood up quickly, suddenly aware of how shabby I must look in my thrift store sweater and jeans, how out of place in this temple of wealth and power. But I squared my shoulders and met his gaze, refusing to be intimidated.

"Samson," I replied, proud that my voice came out steady.

I opened my mouth to launch into my prepared speech, ready to unleash all the anger I'd been cultivating since last night. Ready to denounce him in front of his employees and customers, to expose him as the heartless predator he was.

But before I could get out a single word, he did something completely unexpected.

He took my hand in his.

His skin was warm, his grip firm but gentle, and I felt the contact like an electric shock running up my arm. Before I could react, before I could even process what was happening, he bowed slightly—actually *bowed*—and brought my knuckles to his lips.

The kiss was soft, brief, barely more than a whisper of contact. But it sent my carefully constructed anger scattering like leaves in the wind.

What the hell is he doing?

I must have looked as confused as I felt, because I saw the corner of his mouth quirk up in what might have been amusement.

"Come up to my office," he said, his voice pitched low enough that only I could hear. "We can talk more privately there."

Before I could protest, before I could remember that I was supposed to be furious with him, he'd tucked my hand into the crook of his arm—a gesture that was somehow both old-fashioned and possessive—and was leading me toward the employee door.

I caught a glimpse of the lobby as we walked away. Every single person was staring at us. The young man who'd fetched Samson looked like he might faint. A woman at one of the tables had her mouth hanging open. Even the other employees were watching with barely concealed curiosity.

And Samson, the bastard, looked completely unruffled. Like escorting women through his bank while the entire staff gawked was something he did every day.

The employee door closed behind us, cutting off the lobby and its audience, and I finally found my voice.

"What was that?" I demanded, pulling my hand free from his arm. "The hand-kissing, the—the performance?"

We were in a hallway now, all sleek lines and muted colors, doors branching off on either side. It was quieter here, more intimate, and I was suddenly very aware that we were alone.

Samson turned to face me, and his expression was impossible to read. "Would you have preferred I let you make a scene in my lobby? I assume that was your plan, based on the way you announced yourself to my staff."

Heat flooded my cheeks. "I wasn't going to make a scene. I was going to tell you exactly what I think of you foreclosing on my grandmother's house."

"Loudly? In front of everyone?" His eyebrow arched. "That's called making a scene, Madison. And while I admire your passion, it wouldn't have helped your grandmother. It would have embarrassed you, disrupted my business, and accomplished nothing except making you feel momentarily satisfied."

I hated that he was right. Hated it with every fiber of my being.

"So instead you... what? Made it look like we're..." I gestured vaguely between us, unable to finish the sentence.

"I made it look like you're someone important," he said simply. "Someone with connections. Someone whose concerns I take seriously enough to see immediately, despite my schedule. Trust me—that display will work in your favor far more than righteous indignation would have."

He turned and continued down the hallway, clearly expecting me to follow. After a moment's hesitation, I did, my anger warring with grudging acknowledgment that his strategy might actually be smarter than mine.

We reached the end of the hallway, where a private elevator waited. Samson pressed the button, and the doors opened immediately.

"After you," he said, gesturing for me to enter.

I stepped inside the elevator, and he followed, the small space suddenly feeling much smaller with both of us in it. The doors slid closed, sealing us in together, and I tried very hard not to notice how good he smelled—something expensive and masculine, cedar and spice and something else I couldn't identify.

"Your office is upstairs?" I asked, needing to break the silence.

"The third floor. I prefer the separation from the daily operations." He pressed the button for the top floor. "It allows me to see the larger picture without getting caught up in the minutiae."

"How convenient," I said, unable to keep the bite out of my voice. "You can foreclose on people's homes without having to look them in the eye."

The elevator began its ascent, smooth and silent, and Samson turned to look at me with an expression I couldn't decipher.

"Is that really what you think I do? Sit in my ivory tower, randomly destroying lives for profit?"

"Aren't you?"

"No, Madison. I run a bank. A successful one, yes, but still a bank. And banks have rules, regulations, contracts that must be honored. Your grandmother signed a mortgage agreement. She agreed to make payments. When those payments stop, there are consequences. That's not cruelty—that's business."

"She had her social security reduced!" The words burst out of me, sharp with frustration. "Through no fault of her own, her income dropped, and now you're punishing her for it!"

"I'm not punishing anyone," he said, and there was something almost sad in his voice. "I'm following the law. If I make exceptions, if I let emotional considerations override financial ones, the entire system collapses. You do understand that, don't you?"

The elevator chimed softly, announcing our arrival at the third floor. The doors opened onto another hallway, this one plushly carpeted, with artwork on the walls that probably cost more than Grandma's mortgage.

"Come," Samson said, stepping out. "Let's have this conversation in my office, where we can sit down and discuss this properly."

CHAPTER 5

The office was stunning.

That was the only word for it—stunning in a way that made my carefully rehearsed anger feel small and inadequate. We'd climbed a short flight of stairs from the elevator, walked down a hallway lined with paintings that belonged in a museum, each one accompanied by a small brass plaque engraved with the artist's name. I recognized a few—Monet, Degas, names I'd learned about in the single art history class I'd taken in college—and tried not to think about how much they must have cost.

Samson stopped outside an open doorway at the end of the hall and extended his left hand in invitation.

I stepped past him and had to physically suppress a gasp.

The office was breathtaking. Elegant seemed too simple a word for it. The centerpiece was an enormous mahogany desk, the wood polished to such a high shine I could see my reflection in its surface. But it was everything else that drew my attention, pulled my gaze in a dozen different directions at once.

Floor-to-ceiling bookshelves lined one wall, filled with leather-bound volumes. A Persian rug—or something equally expensive and antique—sprawled across the center of the room in rich burgundies and golds, its surface so plush and inviting that I had an absurd urge to take off my shoes and walk barefoot across it. A sitting area near the windows featured leather chairs that matched the ones in the lobby, arranged around a low glass table.

And on the far wall, a fireplace. An actual fireplace, complete with an ornate mantle and what looked like genuine marble surround. It was dark now, unlit, but I could imagine how it would look crackling with flames on a winter evening, casting warm light across the expensive furniture and priceless art.

This wasn't an office. This was a carefully curated display of wealth and power, designed to remind anyone who entered exactly who they were dealing with.

"Have a seat," Samson said, his voice pulling me from my stunned observation.

He moved to pull out one of the chairs positioned in front of his desk—not the intimidating leather throne behind it, but the guest chairs, upholstered in soft charcoal fabric. The gesture was oddly gentlemanly, formal in a way that felt like it belonged to a different era.

I sat, hyper-aware of his proximity as he guided the chair forward. His hand touched my shoulder, the contact brief but somehow intimate, his fingers lingering for just a moment before he withdrew and circled around to his own seat.

The chair was incredibly comfortable. Of course it was. Everything in this office was designed for comfort and intimidation in equal measure—make your guests feel pampered while reminding them that they were in the presence of someone far more successful than they could ever hope to be.

I watched Samson settle into his chair with fluid grace, and for a moment, I understood exactly how my mother had fallen for him. He was magnetic in a way I'd never fully appreciated before. Handsome, yes, but it was more than that. It was the confidence, the way he commanded space without seeming to try, the intelligence in those dark eyes that suggested he was always three moves ahead in a game you didn't even know you were playing.

The Wolf. The nickname suited him perfectly.

"To what do I owe the pleasure of your visit today?" he asked, his tone polite, almost playful.

I'd almost forgotten why I was here. Staring at him across that massive desk, taking in the perfect tailoring of his suit and the way his eyes seemed to see right through me, I felt my carefully prepared speech dissolving like sugar in water.

Don't be stupid, I berated myself silently. *He knows exactly why you're here. Stop letting him charm you.*

"Grandmother's house," I said, forcing the words out. I paused, trying to harden my resolve, to remember the anger that had fueled me all night and all morning. Why was it so much harder now? Why did being in this room, in his presence, make everything feel different?

"Ah, yes." He leaned back in his chair, steepling his fingers in a gesture I recognized from countless movies. "I thought that might warrant a phone call from you, perhaps. I didn't anticipate a personal visit."

"Are you completely heartless?" The question burst out before I could temper it with diplomacy. "She's an elderly woman living on social security. Where exactly do you expect her to go?"

Samson's expression didn't change. That charming smile remained fixed in place, professional and impenetrable. "I have a business to run, Madison. If I forgave everyone's debt simply because their circumstances became difficult, I'd have to close this bank down within a month."

"You don't exactly seem to be hurting," I shot back, gesturing at the opulent office around us. "What difference would it make if you let this one go? I'm sure you make more than what she owes in a single day."

His smile widened, gaining an edge that was almost predatory. "Come now, give me more credit than that. I make what your grandmother owes in an hour."

I snorted, crossing my arms over my chest. Whatever charm he'd been wielding was rapidly fading as my anger rekindled, burning away the haze of intimidation. "If you think that impresses me, it doesn't. And stop changing the subject."

"I didn't change the subject," he countered smoothly. "You're the one who brought up my finances. I was merely correcting your underestimation."

I opened my mouth to argue, then snapped it shut again. Damn him, he was right. He was deflecting by letting me deflect, using my own tactics against me. I glared at him across the desk, trying to marshal my thoughts into something coherent.

"Why can't you just forgive her debt?" I demanded. "Her social security was cut through no fault of her own. She can barely afford groceries and her medications, let alone a mortgage payment. She's not trying to cheat you. She's not irresponsible. She's just—she's drowning, and you're holding her head under water."

"If I did it for one person, everyone else would expect the same treatment," Samson said, and for the first time, there was something almost regretful in his tone. "Word travels fast in a town this size. If I forgive your grandmother's debt, by next week I'll have fifty people in my lobby demanding the same consideration. Each with their own compelling story, their own difficult circumstances. Where do I draw the line, Madison? Who deserves mercy and who doesn't?"

"You draw the line at basic human decency!" My voice was rising now, frustration bleeding into desperation. "You draw the line at not throwing a seventy-three-year-old woman out of her home!"

"The debt has to be repaid," he said simply. "Those are the terms of the contract she signed. I cannot make exceptions, regardless of my personal feelings on the matter."

It felt impossible to argue with him. Every point I made, he countered with cold logic that I couldn't dispute. I bit the inside of my cheek hard enough to taste copper, my mind racing for some angle I hadn't considered, some leverage I didn't have.

"How much does she owe?" I asked finally, though I had no idea why I was even asking. It wasn't like I had money to offer him. I could barely keep my own bills paid.

"With or without late fees?" He asked it casually, like we were discussing the weather.

"Seriously?" I could feel my control slipping, the professional veneer I'd been trying to maintain cracking apart. "Just tell me the fucking amount."

"My, my." He laughed, a rich sound that should have been pleasant but instead felt mocking. "You're even more feisty than your mother ever was. I like that."

He leaned forward, placing his elbows on the pristine surface of his desk and clasping his fingers together in front of him. The gesture brought him closer, made the space between us feel smaller, more intimate.

"I'll tell you what," he said, his voice taking on a negotiating tone. "Since you came all this way, since you're family—of a sort—I'll waive the late fees entirely. I'll even round the balance down to make the numbers simpler."

Hope flared in my chest, sudden and painful.

"She owes fifty thousand dollars."

The hope gutted itself, leaving me hollow.

Fifty thousand dollars. The number was so astronomical it didn't even feel real. Who had that kind of money just sitting around? Well, besides the man sitting across from me, who probably spent that much on suits in a year.

I must have looked as shell-shocked as I felt, because Samson leaned back in his chair and tapped his chin thoughtfully, studying me like I was a particularly interesting puzzle.

"I don't suppose you have that kind of money?" he asked, and there was something almost knowing in his tone. Like he already knew the answer and was just being polite by asking.

"Of course not!" The words came out sharper than I intended, edged with humiliation and frustration. "If I had fifty thousand dollars lying around, I wouldn't be living in a house with no heat. I wouldn't be working myself to death at a hotel that treats me like disposable labor. And maybe—"

I cut myself off, but too late. The words were already halfway out.

"Maybe what?" Samson prompted gently.

"Nothing. It doesn't matter."

"Madison." The way he said my name made it sound like a command, soft but unyielding. "Maybe what?"

The fight drained out of me all at once, leaving me exhausted and raw. "Maybe my boyfriend wouldn't have cheated on me if I wasn't such a broke, pathetic failure," I finished quietly, staring at my bandaged hands in my lap.

The words hung in the air between us. I wanted to take them back, to swallow them down and pretend I'd never said them. Why had I said that? And to him, of all people? My mother's ex-husband, a man I barely knew, who I was supposed to be fighting right now instead of spilling my personal disasters all over his expensive office.

When I finally worked up the courage to look at him, his expression had changed entirely. The charming smile was gone, replaced by something I couldn't quite identify. Concern? Anger?

"Your boyfriend cheated on you?" His voice was low, carefully controlled, but there was an edge to it that hadn't been there before.

"Ex-boyfriend," I corrected automatically. "As of last night."

"Madison, I'm—" He paused, seeming to choose his words carefully. "I'm sorry. That's... that's inexcusable behavior. Particularly if his reasons were as shallow as you're suggesting."

The sincerity in his voice caught me off guard. I'd expected mockery, or worse, indifference. Not this quiet sympathy that made my throat tighten with suppressed emotion.

"Would you like me to have a conversation with him?" Samson continued. "I can be very... persuasive when I want to be."

The offer was so unexpected, so far outside the bounds of our relationship—whatever that relationship even was—that I couldn't help but let out a weak laugh.

"What, you're going to threaten to foreclose on his house too?"

"If necessary." He wasn't smiling. "Though I was thinking something more along the lines of a frank discussion about respect and consequences. The kind of discussion that tends to stick with people."

Despite everything—my anger at him, my desperation about Grandma's situation, my heartbreak over Jason—I felt something warm kindle in my chest at the protective tone in his voice. It was absurd. This man was foreclosing on my grandmother's house, and here he was offering to defend my honor like some kind of knight in a designer suit.

"No," I said firmly. "Thank you, but no. Jason's not worth the effort. Just... forget I said anything about it."

"Are you certain?"

"Yes." I forced myself to meet his gaze again, trying to project a confidence I didn't feel. "I don't need you to fight my battles for me. I just need you to have a heart where my grandmother is concerned."

We looked at each other across the desk, and I could see him processing, calculating, that sharp mind working through angles I couldn't even guess at.

"Are you still working at that hotel?" he asked suddenly, shifting topics so smoothly it took me a moment to adjust. "The one on Sunset Court?"

"Yeah." I answered warily, unsure where this was going. I hated that job with every fiber of my being, but I wasn't about to admit that to him. Wasn't about to give him any more ammunition than he already had.

"Do you enjoy it there?"

I wanted to say yes. Intended to say yes, to maintain some shred of dignity and independence. But when I opened my mouth, what came out was a weak, defeated, "No."

Damn it!

What was it about him that made it so hard to maintain my defenses? He had this way of disarming you, of making you feel comfortable even when you knew you shouldn't be. Like he genuinely cared about the answer, when logically I knew he was just gathering information, finding weak points.

I swallowed hard against the lump forming in my throat and raised my eyes to meet his. Time to play the only card I had left—complete, honest desperation.

"I've never asked you for anything," I said quietly. "Not when Mom divorced you, not when she left town, not ever. I've never called you, never shown up at your office, never treated you like family even though technically you were married to my mother for five years. I've kept my distance and let you live your life."

Samson was silent, watching me with those penetrating eyes.

"All I want," I continued, hearing my voice crack slightly, "is for you to forgive her debt. Please. Don't kick her out of the only home she has. She raised me in that house after my dad died. She took care of my mother when no one else would. She's the kindest, most generous person I know, and she doesn't deserve this."

The Wolf sighed, a long exhale that seemed to carry weight.

For a moment, I thought he was going to give in. Thought I saw something soften in his expression, some crack in the professional armor he wore so perfectly.

"A debt has to be repaid," he said again, but this time his voice was quieter. He leaned forward, and there was something in his eyes that made me uncomfortable—something that took the warmth out of the room and replaced it with a different kind of heat entirely. "However... I'm sure we can work something out."

Relief and wariness warred in my chest. "Like what?"

He smiled, and it wasn't the charming smile from before. This was something else entirely.

"Let me make you my mistress."

CHAPTER 6

The words hung in the air. For a moment, I wasn't sure I'd heard him correctly. My brain refused to process what he'd just said, kept trying to reinterpret it into something less shocking, less impossible.

"What?" The word came out as barely a whisper.

"You heard me." Samson stood, moving around the desk with predatory grace. He perched on the edge of it, directly in front of me, close enough that I had to tilt my head back to maintain eye contact. "Become my mistress. Give me your time, your company, your... attention. In return, I'll forgive your grandmother's debt. All fifty thousand dollars of it, gone. She can live in that house for the rest of her life without owing me a single penny."

My mouth opened and closed soundlessly. I felt like I'd been punched in the stomach, all the air driven from my lungs.

"You can't be serious," I finally managed.

"I'm always serious when it comes to business, Madison. And make no mistake—this would be a business arrangement." He crossed his arms over his chest, the movement making the fabric of his suit jacket strain across his shoulders. "You need money. I have money. You need your grandmother's debt forgiven. I have the power to forgive it. You have something I want. It's a simple transaction."

"Simple?" I stood up abruptly, my chair scraping against the floor. "You're proposing that I—that we—you want me to prostitute myself to save my grandmother's house!"

"Prostitution is such an ugly word." His tone was maddeningly calm. "I prefer to think of it as a mutually beneficial arrangement between two consenting adults."

I stared at him, my mind reeling. This couldn't be happening. This morning, I'd woken up planning to give him a piece of my mind about his heartless business practices. Now he was calmly proposing that I become his—his what? Sex toy?

"I would never—" I started, but he interrupted.

"Before you refuse," he said, raising one hand, "think carefully. Think about your grandmother, about that house she loves." Each word was a precision strike, hitting exactly where it would hurt most. Samson continued, his voice dropping lower, becoming almost hypnotic. "I'm offering you a way to solve your grandmother's problem."

He stood, closing the distance between us until he was close enough that I could smell his cologne, feel the heat radiating from his body.

"All you have to do," he murmured, "is say yes."

I stood there, trapped between the chair behind me and the Wolf in front of me, and felt the world tilting sideways. Everything I thought I knew about this man, about myself, about what I was willing to do—all of it was being called into question.

"I need to think," I heard myself say, the words coming from somewhere far away. "I need—I can't—"

"Of course." He stepped back, giving me space to breathe, and the professional mask slipped back into place as smoothly as if it had never left. "Take all the time you need. Well," he amended with a slight smile, "take up to thirty days. That's when the foreclosure proceedings begin, after all."

The casual cruelty of the timeline made me flinch.

"Think about it, Madison," Samson said, moving back around his desk to reclaim his seat. "Really think about it. And when you've made your decision, you know where to find me."

I nodded mutely, not trusting myself to speak, and turned toward the door on legs that felt like they might give out at any moment.

"Oh, and Madison?"

I paused at the doorway, looking back.

His expression was unreadable, somewhere between amusement and something darker. "I do hope you'll choose wisely. I'd hate to see your grandmother lose her home over something as simple as pride."

I fled.

There was no other word for it. I practically ran down that hallway with its expensive paintings and plush carpet, jabbed the elevator button repeatedly until the doors opened, and stood trembling in the corner as it descended back to the lobby.

When the doors opened, I kept my head down and walked as quickly as I could through the still-busy bank, ignoring the curious stares, ignoring the young employee who'd announced me earlier. I burst through the glass doors into the parking lot and made it to my car before the shaking got so bad I had to lean against the hood to stay upright.

Let me make you my mistress.

The words echoed in my head, impossible to escape.

I got into my car, started the engine, and sat there for a long moment, staring at the Den's elegant facade.

Samson Lang had just propositioned me. Had offered to essentially buy me in exchange for my grandmother's freedom.

And the worst part, the absolutely terrifying part that made my stomach churn and my heart race, was that some small, desperate part of me was actually considering it.

I sat in my car in the parking lot of the Den for what felt like hours but was probably only twenty minutes, my hands gripping the steering wheel so tightly my knuckles had gone white.

Let me make you my mistress.

The words kept echoing in my head, impossible to escape, impossible to reconcile with the reality of my situation. This morning, I'd been planning to shame him in front of his employees. Now I was sitting here seriously considering whether I was willing to sell myself to save my grandmother's house.

I should have stormed out of his office with a string of curses, should have told him exactly where he could shove his proposition. But the image of Grandma's face when she'd tried to hide how scared she was about the eviction kept rising in my mind. The way her hands had trembled slightly as she'd assured me everything would be fine, even though we both knew it wouldn't be.

Fifty thousand dollars. Three months of missed payments that had snowballed into an impossible sum. And Samson was offering to make it all disappear.

For a price.

I pressed my forehead against the steering wheel and tried to think clearly through the chaos of emotions swirling in my chest. Shame, desperation, anger—and underneath it all, something I didn't want to acknowledge. A flutter of something that felt uncomfortably like excitement when I thought about his eyes on me, his voice dropping low as he'd stood so close I could feel the heat of his body.

Stop it, I told myself firmly. *You're not attracted to him. You're just desperate and vulnerable and he's taking advantage of that.*

But even as I thought it, I knew it wasn't entirely true. Samson was handsome in a way that made my hindbrain sit up and take notice, regardless of how much my rational mind wanted to hate him. Power was attractive, confidence was attractive, and he had both in spades.

My phone buzzed in my purse, making me jump. I fumbled for it, half-expecting it to be Marcus somehow, but it was just a notification from the hotel asking if I could pick up an extra shift tomorrow. The manager didn't even bother to phrase it as a question—

just an expectation that I'd say yes because I always said yes, because I needed the money too badly to refuse.

I stared at the notification for a long moment, then turned off my phone entirely.

I couldn't think about this here, in the parking lot where anyone could see me. I needed space, needed to process, needed to figure out if I was actually considering this insane proposition or if the stress had finally broken something fundamental in my brain.

I started the car and drove home on autopilot, my mind a million miles away.

CHAPTER 7

Three days later, I found myself standing in my kitchen at two in the morning, unable to sleep, staring at the eviction notice I'd stolen from Grandma's house.

Thirty days. She had thirty days to come up with four thousand dollars or lose everything.

I'd spent the last seventy-two hours running through every possible alternative. I'd called every bank in the area asking about loans—denied, denied, denied. My credit was garbage, I had no collateral, no co-signer. I'd looked into selling my car, but it was worth maybe a thousand dollars on a good day, and I needed it to get to work anyway.

I'd even swallowed my pride and called my mother in Hawaii.

That conversation had been short and brutal. She'd listened to my explanation about Grandma's situation with what sounded like genuine concern, right up until I asked if she could help.

"Honey, you know Richard and I keep our finances separate," she'd said, and I could hear the champagne brunch in her voice, the background chatter of her wealthy new life. "And he's very particular about loans to family. It gets messy. I'm sure your grandmother will figure something out. She always does."

Then she'd made an excuse about a spa appointment and hung up.

I'd sat there staring at my phone for ten minutes, trying to process the fact that my mother—the woman who'd lived in that house, who'd been raised by the same grandmother now facing eviction—couldn't be bothered to help.

Wouldn't be bothered, more accurately. She could help. She just didn't want to.

Which left me back where I'd started: staring at Samson's business card, the one he'd slipped into my hand as I'd fled his office three days ago.

When you've made your decision, you know where to find me.

I picked up my phone and scrolled to his contact before I could second-guess myself.

My finger hovered over the call button for a long moment.

Was I really going to do this? Was I really so desperate that I'd agree to become some rich man's plaything in exchange for money?

The eviction notice crinkled in my other hand, and I thought about Grandma knitting in her chair, surrounded by a lifetime of memories and love, about to lose it all because the system was rigged against people like her.

I hit the call button.

It rang three times before his voice came through, smooth and unsurprised even though it was the middle of the night.

"Madison. I was wondering when you'd call."

"I want to talk," I said, forcing my voice to stay steady. "About your... proposition."

"Of course. Can you come to my office tomorrow? Say, ten o'clock?"

"I work tomorrow."

"Call in sick." It wasn't a suggestion. "This is more important than scrubbing hotel toilets."

I should have been offended by the casual dismissal of my job, but he wasn't wrong. This was more important. This was everything.

"Fine. Ten o'clock."

"I'll see you then, Madison. And Madison?" His voice dropped lower, became almost intimate. "I'm glad you called. I think we're going to work very well together."

He hung up before I could respond, leaving me standing in my dark kitchen with my heart pounding and the terrible certainty that I'd just crossed a line I could never uncross.

I didn't sleep for the rest of the night. By the time I pulled into the Den's parking lot the next morning, I was running on adrenaline and three cups of bad coffee, my nerves stretched so thin I felt like I might shatter at the slightest touch.

The lobby was busy with the morning rush—people depositing checks, discussing mortgage terms, all the normal business of a bank. I walked through it all in a daze, barely registering the curious glances from the impeccably dressed staff.

The same young man from before appeared at my elbow almost immediately, his professional smile firmly in place.

"Ms. Carter. Mr. Lang is expecting you. Please, follow me."

He led me through the employee door, up the stairs, down the hallway with its expensive art. Each step felt surreal, like I was watching myself from outside my own body. Was I really doing this? Was this really happening?

We reached Samson's office. The young man knocked twice and waited for the call to enter before opening the door.

"Ms. Carter, sir," he announced, then stepped aside to let me pass.

Samson was standing by the window, backlit by the morning sun in a way that made him look almost ethereal. He turned as I entered, and the smile that crossed his face was genuine—pleased, almost warm.

"Madison. Thank you for coming." He dismissed the employee with a small gesture, and the door clicked shut behind me, leaving us alone. "Please, sit down. Can I get you anything? Coffee? Water?"

"No, thank you." I remained standing, my arms crossed defensively over my chest. "Let's just... let's talk about this."

"Of course." He moved to sit on the edge of his desk, that same position from before that put us almost at eye level. Close, but not threatening. "I assume you're here because you've given serious consideration to my offer?"

"I want to know the details first." My voice sounded steadier than I felt. "Before I agree to anything, I need to know exactly what you're expecting."

"Fair enough." He nodded approvingly. "I appreciate a woman who negotiates terms. It shows intelligence."

"Don't patronize me."

"I wouldn't dream of it." His smile widened slightly. "All right, here's what I'm proposing: I'll forgive your grandmother's debt in its entirety—fifty thousand dollars, all late fees waived. In exchange, you'll give me three days of your time."

"Three days," I repeated slowly. "And in those three days, you expect..."

"Complete compliance," he said simply. "Three days where I can do whatever I want with you, however I want. No limitations, no refusals. You'll submit to my desires entirely."

Heat flooded my face, but I forced myself to maintain eye contact. "And if I refuse? If you ask for something I'm not comfortable with?"

"Then the deal is void immediately, and foreclosure proceedings begin the next day." His tone was matter-of-fact, businesslike. "Think of it as a contract with very specific terms. You either fulfill those terms completely, or the contract is nullified."

I wanted to tell him to go to hell. Wanted to storm out with my dignity intact. But the image of Grandma's face kept me rooted in place.

"What's the catch?" I asked instead. "This seems too straightforward for someone with your reputation."

Samson brought his hand to his heart in an exaggerated gesture of offense. "You wound me, Madison. There's no catch. It's a simple deal for a simple situation."

There was nothing simple about this, and we both knew it.

I tried to imagine it—him touching me, his hands on my body, giving myself over to him completely. The thought sent a confusing mix of anxiety and something else through my system. Something that felt disturbingly like anticipation.

I shoved the feeling down ruthlessly. This wasn't about attraction or desire. This was a business transaction, just like he'd said. I was trading my body for my grandmother's security, and I needed to keep that clear in my mind.

"There will be a written agreement?" I asked, trying to sound professional, like this was a normal negotiation and not the most surreal conversation of my life.

"Of course. Though the wording will need to be carefully constructed for... legal reasons." He stood and moved behind his desk, pulling out a folder. "I've already had my attorney draft something. You're welcome to have it reviewed by your own lawyer before signing."

"I don't have a lawyer," I admitted. "I can barely afford groceries."

Something flickered across his face—sympathy, maybe, or pity. I wasn't sure which would be worse.

"Then I'll walk you through it myself, line by line. I want you to understand exactly what you're agreeing to." He opened the folder and pulled out several pages of dense legal text. "The basic structure is that I'm forgiving the debt as a personal favor, with no monetary compensation required. In exchange, you're agreeing to provide... consulting services to the bank over a period of three non-consecutive days."

"Consulting services," I repeated, almost laughing at the absurd euphemism.

"Standard language for discretionary payments." He had the grace to look slightly amused. "We can't exactly put 'sexual favors' in a legally binding contract."

I lowered my head, staring at my bandaged hands in my lap. The scrapes from my bicycle accident were healing well, the bandages smaller now, but they served as a reminder of how quickly everything in my life had spiraled out of control.

Three days ago, I'd been worried about my car and my cheating boyfriend. Now I was negotiating the terms of essentially prostituting myself to save my grandmother's house.

But what choice did I have? Really, what choice?

I'd already made my decision. Probably made it the moment Samson had first proposed this insane arrangement, if I was being honest with myself. Everything since then had just been me working up the courage to admit it.

Still, I let him wait. Let the silence stretch between us while I pretended to think it over, maintaining some illusion of dignity and agency. Samson seemed content to let me have that fiction, drumming his fingers lightly on the desk while I processed.

Finally, I looked up and met his gaze directly.

"I'll do it."

The smile that spread across his face was triumphant, almost predatory. There was a gleam in his dark eyes that hadn't been there before—satisfaction, anticipation, something that made my stomach flip with nerves and unwanted excitement.

"Excellent," he said, pulling the contract toward him. "I'll have this finalized today. Once we've both signed, we can schedule our first... appointment."

The word hung in the air, clinical and cold, and I tried not to think too hard about what these "appointments" would entail.

"Where?" I heard myself ask. "A hotel? One of your houses?"

His eyebrow arched. "No. We'll meet right here, in my office."

I stared at him, certain I'd misheard. "You want to—here? In your office? Won't someone hear us?"

"Bank business has to be conducted at the bank," he said with a slight shrug, as if this were perfectly reasonable. "As for being heard, you don't need to worry about that. I'll make sure the surrounding offices are empty on the days you visit. My assistant knows not to disturb me during blocked time. We'll have complete privacy."

The casual way he said it suggested this wasn't the first time he'd used his office for purposes beyond standard banking operations. The thought should have disgusted me. Instead, I felt that unwanted flutter of excitement again, imagining what it would be like to be here with him, to let him—

Clear mind, I reminded myself sharply. *This is business. Just business.*

But even as I thought it, I knew I was lying to myself.

The contract was finalized by the end of the day. Samson called me at six o'clock to let me know it was ready for signing.

I drove back to the Den after my shift at the hotel—I'd gone to work after all, unable to sit at home with my thoughts—and found Samson waiting for me in his office. The building was mostly empty now, just a skeleton crew of security and cleaning staff.

The contract was surprisingly straightforward, once you stripped away the legal jargon. He would forgive the fifty-thousand-dollar debt. I would provide "consulting services" on three separate occasions, dates and times to be determined at his discretion with at least twenty-four hours notice.

"What if I have to work?" I asked as I read that particular clause.

"Call in sick. Take a personal day. Make it work." His tone left no room for argument. "When I call, you come. That's part of the agreement."

I swallowed hard and kept reading.

The contract was for six months from the date of signing. If I failed to fulfill any of the three required appointments, or if I refused any request during those appointments, the debt forgiveness would be revoked and the foreclosure would immediately happen.

"Six months?" I looked up at him. "Why such a long window?"

"Because I'm a busy man, and I want the flexibility to schedule our time together when it's convenient for me." He was watching me carefully, gauging my reaction. "Is that a problem?"

It meant six months of not knowing when he'd call, six months of anxiety and anticipation. But it also meant Grandma would be safe, at least for that period.

"No," I said quietly. "Not a problem."

There were other clauses—confidentiality agreements, stipulations that I couldn't discuss the terms of our arrangement with anyone, provisions for what would happen if either of us died or became incapacitated before the contract was fulfilled. It was thorough, almost obsessively detailed, covering contingencies I hadn't even thought to consider.

At the bottom were signature lines for both of us, and spaces for a witness and a notary.

"My attorney already signed as witness," Samson explained, pointing to the elegant signature. "And I have a notary on call. She's waiting outside whenever you're ready."

This was it. The point of no return.

I picked up the expensive fountain pen he'd laid out and signed my name, the ink flowing smooth and black across the paper. My handwriting looked shaky next to his bold, confident signature, but it was done.

The notary was called in—an older woman who looked bored and professional, stamped the document without commentary, and left without meeting my eyes. Either she didn't know what the contract really entailed, or she knew and didn't care.

Samson placed the contract in a locked drawer of his desk and pocketed the key.

"I'll keep the original here. You'll receive a copy by courier tomorrow." He stood and extended his hand across the desk. "Congratulations, Madison. We have a deal."

I shook his hand, feeling the warmth and strength of his grip, and tried to ignore the way my pulse quickened at the contact.

"When?" I asked. "When will you call me for the first... appointment?"

His smile was slow and devastating. "Soon. I'll let you know at least twenty-four hours in advance, as stipulated. Beyond that..." He shrugged. "I like to keep things spontaneous. Keeps the anticipation alive."

I nodded mutely and turned to leave, but his voice stopped me at the door.

"Madison?"

I looked back.

"I'm looking forward to this," he said simply. "To our time together. I think you will be too, once you stop fighting it."

I fled before he could see the truth in my eyes—that part of me was already looking forward to it, and that terrified me more than anything.

CHAPTER 8

Samson called me almost a week later.

The waiting had been torture. I'd spent every day jumping at every phone notification, every unknown number. My nights were restless, filled with dreams I didn't want to examine too closely—dreams where Samson's hands were on my skin, his voice in my ear, his body pressing mine into expensive sheets.

I'd tried to distract myself with work, with helping Grandma around her house, with anything that would keep my mind occupied. But the anticipation built anyway, coiling tighter and tighter in my chest until I felt like I might snap.

I still hadn't told Grandma about the arrangement. Samson had been clear that if I refused him anything during our appointments, the deal would be void immediately. Since I wasn't entirely certain what he might ask of me, it seemed premature to tell her the house was safe.

Better to wait until all three days were complete, until the debt was truly forgiven.

That's what I told myself, anyway. The truth was I was ashamed, and I didn't want to see the disappointment in her eyes if she found out what I'd done.

When his call finally came, I was at home, fresh from the shower, wearing my most comfortable pajamas and trying to convince myself to eat something. His name lit up my phone screen, and my heart immediately kicked into overdrive.

"Hello?"

"Madison." Just the sound of his voice sent shivers down my spine. "Tomorrow at three o'clock sharp. Don't be late."

"I—okay. Yes. Three o'clock."

"Good girl." The approval in his voice did things to me I didn't want to acknowledge. "I'll see you then."

He hung up before I could respond, leaving me standing in my kitchen with my phone pressed to my ear and my entire body thrumming with nervous energy.

I barely slept that night. Every time I closed my eyes, I saw Samson's face, felt phantom touches on my skin, heard his voice commanding me to—

I forced the thoughts away and checked the clock. Again. Still hours until morning.

The next day, I arrived at the Den's parking lot at two o'clock. An hour early, but I couldn't stand being at home anymore, couldn't handle the waiting.

I sat in my car watching the clock on my dashboard tick forward with agonizing slowness. My hands were shaking. My heart was racing. I felt like I might throw up or pass out or both.

You can still leave, a small voice in my head whispered. *You can drive away right now and never come back.*

But I couldn't. Grandma's house hung in the balance, and I'd signed a contract. I'd made a deal.

I checked my appearance in the rearview mirror for the hundredth time. I'd dressed carefully—nothing too provocative, but nice. A simple dress in deep blue that hugged my curves without being overtly sexual. Minimal makeup. Hair pulled back in a neat ponytail.

I wasn't sure what Samson expected me to wear, but this felt like a safe middle ground.

At 2:55, I couldn't stand it anymore. I got out of the car and walked toward the bank on legs that felt like they might give out at any moment.

The lobby was moderately busy with afternoon customers. I scanned the area for the young man who'd helped me before, but he was nowhere in sight. Instead, a woman approached me—mid-thirties, blonde, with the same polished perfection as all of Samson's employees.

"How can I help you today?" she asked cheerfully.

"I have an appointment with Mr. Lang," I managed, proud that my voice came out steady.

Her smile didn't waver, but something flickered in her eyes. Knowledge? Judgment? I couldn't tell.

"Of course. Right this way, please."

She led me toward the employee door, and I became hyperaware of eyes on me. Was I imagining it, or were people staring? Did they know? Had Marcus told his staff about our arrangement?

Don't be paranoid, I told myself. *You're just another client meeting with the bank president.*

But the woman's sideways glance as we climbed the stairs suggested she knew I was something more than that.

We reached Samson's office door, and she knocked twice, then waited for a moment before opening it without receiving a response.

"He'll be with you shortly," she said, stepping aside to let me enter. "I believe he left something for you on his desk. Make yourself comfortable."

Then she was gone, closing the door behind her with a soft click that sounded unnaturally loud in the quiet office.

I stood frozen for a moment, taking in the space. It looked exactly as I remembered—the expensive desk, the plush rug, the fireplace, the bookshelves. But now it felt different, charged with potential and promise.

He'll be with you shortly.

The phrasing echoed in my mind. Why had she knocked if Samson wasn't even here? And why did her smile suggest she knew exactly what was about to happen in this office?

I shook off the paranoid thoughts and noticed the envelope on the desk, my name written across it in elegant cursive script. The handwriting was too perfect to be Samson's—probably his assistant's work—but seeing my name rendered so beautifully made this feel even more surreal.

With trembling hands, I picked up the envelope and opened it.

Inside was a letter and a soft black blindfold made of what felt like silk.

The letter contained only nine words, written in bold, masculine handwriting that was definitely Samson's:

Get naked. Put this on. Lie on the rug.

My knees went weak. Heat flooded through me, pooling low in my belly, and I had to grip the edge of the desk to steady myself.

This was really happening.

I looked at the windows, suddenly aware of how exposed I was. But Samson's office was on the third floor, and the windows faced away from other buildings. No one would be able to see in unless they were in a helicopter.

Still, the idea of stripping naked in what was essentially a public building made my skin prickle with nervousness and something that felt disturbingly like excitement.

If you refuse me anything, the deal is off.

His words echoed in my mind, a reminder of what was at stake. Grandma's house. Her security. Everything.

I looked at the blindfold in my hand, then at the plush rug in the center of the room. This was what I'd agreed to. What I'd signed a contract promising to do. My hands moved to the zipper of my dress almost of their own accord.

The fabric slid down my body and pooled at my feet. I stepped out of it carefully, folding it and placing it on one of the guest chairs. My bra followed, then my underwear, until I was standing completely naked in Samson Lang's office, goosebumps rising on my skin from the air conditioning and nervous anticipation.

I picked up the blindfold with shaking hands.

Part of me wanted to laugh at the absurdity of this—me, Madison Carter, who worked at a budget hotel and drove a car held together with duct tape and prayer, about to lie naked on a rug that probably cost more than six months of my rent, waiting for a man who could buy and sell me without thinking twice.

But another part of me—a part I didn't want to examine too closely—was thrumming with anticipation. Wanting this. Wanting *him*.

I walked to the rug, feeling the soft fibers against my bare feet. It was as luxurious as it looked, thick and plush, the kind of surface that begged you to sink into it.

I secured the blindfold over my eyes, making sure it was tight enough not to slip but not so tight it was uncomfortable. The world went dark, and my other senses immediately heightened. I could hear the subtle hum of the building's HVAC system, could smell Samson's cologne lingering in the air, could feel every brush of air against my naked skin.

Slowly, carefully, I lowered myself to the rug and lay on my back, my arms at my sides.

And waited.

The vulnerability of my position hit me all at once. I was naked, blindfolded, completely at Samson's mercy in his private office. If he wanted to photograph me, share images with others, humiliate me in ways I couldn't even imagine—I'd have no way to stop him, no way to even see it coming.

But the contract had been explicit about confidentiality. And despite his ruthless business reputation, I had the sense that Samson valued his word.

Or maybe I was just desperately rationalizing my way through this insane situation.

I heard the door open and my heart slammed against my ribs.

Footsteps crossed the floor, bypassing me entirely. I heard the soft whisper of curtains being drawn, blocking out what little natural light might have made it through my blindfold. Then the sound of a drawer opening and closing—what was he getting? What did he have planned?

The footsteps approached, stopped somewhere near my feet.

"On your knees."

CHAPTER 9

I swallowed hard against the lump in my throat and shifted position, moving from lying on my back to kneeling. My knees sank into the plush rug as I waited, every nerve ending in my body hyperaware, attuned to Samson's presence somewhere in the darkness beyond my blindfold.

Was this what he wanted? For me to kneel before him like some kind of supplicant? The image sent a confusing rush of heat through my body—shame and arousal tangled together until I couldn't separate one from the other.

"Not like that," his voice came from somewhere to my right, closer than I'd expected.

I raised my eyebrows questioningly, though I knew he couldn't see the gesture behind the blindfold. My hands fidgeted against my thighs, uncertain.

"Get on all fours."

The command was delivered in that same dark, authoritative tone, and my body responded before my mind could fully process it. The walls of my pussy clenched involuntarily at the mental image his words conjured—Samson behind me, taking me from behind like an animal. The Wolf claiming his prey.

Heat flooded through me, my arousal growing with each passing second. I did as he said, placing my palms flat against the soft fibers of the rug and turning so my ass faced where I thought he was standing. I kept my knees close together deliberately, a small act of defiance. If he wanted to see my pussy, I wanted to hear him demand it.

Silence filled the office.

I stayed frozen in position, my muscles beginning to protest as seconds stretched into what felt like minutes. My arms trembled slightly from the sustained tension. My knees started to ache where they pressed into the rug. Just as I opened my mouth to ask what he was doing, whether I'd done something wrong—

A sharp, stinging pain exploded across my right ass cheek.

I gasped, the sound tearing from my throat involuntarily. The pain had come so suddenly, so unexpectedly, that I'd barely registered the sharp *crack* of impact that preceded it.

The initial sting began to fade into a burning sensation that spread across my skin like fire. I could feel the exact outline of whatever had struck me—not his hand, something else. A belt? A riding crop? My mind raced through possibilities while my body processed the aftermath.

I was going to bruise. I knew it with certainty, could already imagine the mark forming where he'd hit me.

Was Samson into BDSM? The thought sent my hopes for a mutually enjoyable experience plummeting. Of course the Wolf wouldn't be interested in mutual pleasure. This was about power, about control, about him taking what he wanted while I endured it.

"I'm going to strike you again," Samson said, his voice maddeningly calm. "And I don't want you to move. Do you understand?"

I gritted my teeth and forced myself to nod, then remembered he wanted verbal responses. "Yes."

"Yes, what?"

Heat flooded my face. "Yes, sir."

"Good girl."

I braced myself this time, every muscle tense in anticipation. When the next strike came—slapping across my left cheek with that same sharp *crack*—the pain wasn't quite as shocking. I'd been expecting it, had steeled myself against it. But I still cried out, the sound somewhere between a gasp and a whimper.

"Who's a good little whore?" Samson asked, and the degrading term should have made me angry, should have made me want to tell him to go fuck himself.

Instead, it sent a bolt of shameful arousal straight to my core.

"I-I am," I struggled to reply, my voice coming out breathless and small.

Two more strikes followed in quick succession, one on each cheek but in different spots from the first blows. The pain layered, building on itself, my entire ass burning with sensation that walked the razor's edge between agony and something else entirely.

"I can't hear you," he said, and there was amusement in his voice now. The bastard was enjoying this.

"I AM!" I shouted, abandoning any pretense of dignity.

"That's better."

I felt him move closer, felt the heat of his body behind me even though he wasn't touching me yet. I clenched my ass cheeks instinctively, bracing for another strike, but instead something soft but firm pressed against my left cheek.

A thrill ran through me as realization dawned.

His cock.

He was rubbing his cock against my burning skin, and the contact sent sparks of sensation through me—pain where he touched the welts he'd created, but also something darker, something that made my pussy clench with need.

Samson slapped his cock against my ass repeatedly, each contact sending a dull flash of pain through my abused flesh. My back arched involuntarily, my body caught between flinching away and pressing closer, seeking more.

"You like this, don't you?" His voice was lower now, rougher. "I know you want to feel this cock inside you. I can see your arousal."

His fingers brushed my mound without warning, and I gasped at the contact. Then he was sliding them along my slit, parting my labia, and I couldn't suppress the moan that escaped me.

I was wet. Soaked, actually. The evidence of my arousal coating his fingers as he explored me with slow, deliberate strokes.

"Oh, yes," he said softly, and I could hear the satisfaction in his voice. "You definitely want my cock. You're drenched for me, you little slut."

The word should have offended me. Should have made me feel cheap and degraded. Instead, it made me wetter.

"You want daddy's cock?" he asked, and the term sent a confusing rush of heat through me. He wasn't my father—wasn't even technically my stepfather anymore—but the taboo implication made my pulse race.

"Yes," I whispered, past the point of pretending otherwise.

"I bet you do."

I felt his cock press between my ass cheeks, the crown hovering at my back entrance. I bit my lip hard, expecting him to push inside, to take my ass without preparation or mercy. The anticipation was almost unbearable—fear and desire mixing until I couldn't tell them apart.

But he just held there, maintaining slight pressure without penetrating. Teasing me with the possibility, letting me feel how close he was to taking that final virginity.

I wanted him to do it. God help me, in that moment I wanted him more than I'd ever wanted anything. The temptation to push back against him, to force the issue and impale myself on his cock, was almost overwhelming.

I was on the verge of doing exactly that when he pulled away.

The denial was so sudden, so unexpected, that I groaned in disappointment before I could stop myself.

The whip—crop, belt, whatever it was—cracked across my lower back with enough force to make stars explode behind my blindfolded eyes.

"Oh my God!" I hissed, my eyes welling with tears from the pain. My fingers gripped the rug so tightly I was surprised I didn't tear the fibers. I breathed rapidly through my nose, desperate for the pain to lessen, to fade to something manageable.

It did, eventually, with agonizing slowness. And as it faded, a strange realization crystallized in my mind: pain seemed to last forever, stretching out each second into an eternity. But pleasure? Pleasure was fleeting, gone almost as soon as you grasped it.

Samson's lips touched my burning flesh, soft and gentle in stark contrast to the violence he'd just inflicted. He ran a trail of kisses from one side of my ass to the other, each one a benediction, an apology, a promise.

His hand pressed against the upper part of my back, guiding me downward, and I followed his lead until my forehead touched the rug. The position left me completely exposed, vulnerable in a way that sent another rush of arousal through my system.

I felt Samson's hands between my thighs, spreading my legs wider apart. Then his face was buried in my ass, and I gasped at the unexpected intimacy of it.

His tongue—warm and wet and sinfully talented—probed the edges of my puckered hole. My legs trembled, both from the sensation and from the strain of holding this position. Every muscle in my body was taut, caught between the instinct to pull away from such intimate contact and the desire to press closer, to demand more.

Lower, I thought desperately. *Eat my pussy.*

I tried to will the thought into his mind through sheer force of desire, but instead of moving to my dripping cunt, his tongue delved deeper into my asshole.

The sensation was unlike anything I'd ever experienced. His tongue was soft and pleasant, but the wetness felt odd, almost wrong. I'd never let anyone do this before— had never even considered it as something I might enjoy.

But I did enjoy it. The realization sent a shock through my system.

I turned my head so the side of my face pressed against the rug and reached back with both hands, spreading my cheeks wider in silent invitation. Offering myself to him more completely.

Samson's tongue drove deeper, working in circles inside me, exploring virgin territory with patient thoroughness. I lost track of time, lost in the strange, overwhelming sensations he was creating. It seemed to end too quickly when he finally pulled back, leaving me empty and aching.

Then I felt his finger at my entrance, pressing inside to replace his tongue.

"Mmm, yeah," I mewled, past caring how desperate I sounded.

He worked his finger in and out, and I was astonished when I felt my orgasm starting to build from such unconventional stimulation. The pressure originated deep in my pussy but worked its way down, my entire lower body lighting up with sensation. My clit began to tingle, swelling with need, and I had to bite down on the rug to muffle my scream as pleasure crashed through me in waves.

My legs were going numb from the sustained position, trembling so violently I was afraid they might give out entirely.

"Who wants to be my cum slut?" Samson asked, his voice rough with his own need.

I released my ass cheeks and pushed my head up from the floor, my entire body still shaking with aftershocks. "Me," I answered, my voice low and husky, barely recognizable as my own. "Come for me."

What was this man doing to me? The thought flitted through my pleasure-hazed mind. *What am I becoming?*

I felt the crown of Samson's cock press against my pussy, and my breath caught in anticipation. Finally. Finally, he was going to fuck me, going to fill me the way I'd been craving since this all started.

But instead of pushing inside, he rubbed the tip up my slit to my ass, then back down again. Up and down, up and down, his pace increasing but never giving me what I needed.

The teasing was exquisite torture. I wanted him inside me, wanted to feel him slide into my wetness and release his seed deep in my body. I moved my hips in concert with his rhythm, trying to encourage him, to show him how much I wanted this.

He grunted, and suddenly his cock wasn't touching me anymore.

Confusion and disappointment warred in my chest. I wanted to rip off the blindfold and look at him, to demand an explanation, but fear of punishment kept me in place.

Something thick and hot splattered onto my lower back, and understanding dawned.

His cum. He was coming on me, not in me.

I heard the wet sounds of him stroking himself, felt more ropes of his release land on my skin—marking me, claiming me, painting me with his pleasure.

For a long moment, there was only the sound of Samson's ragged breathing and my own confused panting. Then I heard him moving around, the rustle of fabric suggesting he was dressing himself.

"Wait until I leave, then get dressed," his voice came, already more composed, the businesslike tone creeping back in. "Your first day is done."

I heard his footsteps cross the floor, heard the door open and close with a soft click.

And then I was alone, kneeling on the rug with his cum cooling on my back, my body still trembling with unfulfilled need, my mind spinning with questions I wasn't sure I wanted answered.

Why hadn't he fucked me?

The question echoed in my head as I slowly peeled off the blindfold, blinking against the sudden light. The office was empty, just as I'd expected. The curtains were still drawn. My clothes were still folded neatly on the chair.

I looked down at myself and saw the evidence of what we'd done—red welts across my ass and lower back, his cum streaking my skin. I should have felt humiliated, degraded, used.

Instead, I felt... confused. Frustrated. And underneath it all, a burning curiosity about what the other two days would bring.

I stood on shaky legs and made my way to the small bathroom attached to Samson's office—of course he had a private bathroom, complete with expensive toiletries and plush towels. I cleaned myself up as best I could, wincing as the warm washcloth touched the welts he'd created.

They were already darkening into bruises, exactly as I'd predicted. I'd have to be careful about how I moved for the next few days, careful not to let anyone see.

As I dressed, I caught my reflection in the mirror and barely recognized the woman staring back at me. My eyes were bright, my cheeks flushed, my lips swollen from biting them. I looked thoroughly debauched, even cleaned up and fully clothed.

I looked like someone who'd just been used for a powerful man's pleasure.

The thought should have made me feel terrible. Instead, it sent a final flutter of arousal through my exhausted body.

I left Samson's office as quietly as I'd entered it, taking the elevator down to the lobby and walking through the bank with my head held high, pretending I was just another client who'd had a perfectly normal meeting.

The blonde woman who'd escorted me up was at a desk near the entrance. She looked up as I passed, and I saw it clearly in her eyes—knowledge. She knew, or at least suspected, what had happened upstairs.

I met her gaze steadily and didn't look away until she did.

Only when I was safely in my car, doors locked and engine running, did I let myself fully process what had just happened.

I'd gone into that office as Madison Carter, struggling hotel maid with a dying car and a mountain of problems.

I'd come out as someone else entirely. Someone who'd let a man whip her, who'd spread herself open for his tongue, who'd begged to be his cum slut.

Someone who was already counting the days until he called again.

I drove home in a daze, my body aching in places I'd never ached before, my mind replaying every moment, every sensation, every degrading word that had somehow transformed into praise.

When I got home, I found a package waiting on my doorstep—the copy of the contract Samson had promised to send. I brought it inside and set it on my kitchen counter without opening it, staring at it like it might bite.

This was real. This was happening. I'd signed away three days of my life to save my grandmother's house, and I'd just lived through the first one.

Two more to go.

My phone buzzed with a text message, and my heart jumped. But it wasn't from Marcus. It was from Grandma, asking if I wanted to come over for dinner.

I stared at the message for a long moment, then typed back a response: *Not tonight. I'm exhausted. Tomorrow?*

Her reply came quickly: *Of course, dear. Get some rest. I love you.*

I love you too, I typed back, and meant it with every fiber of my being.

This was why I was doing this. For her. For the woman who'd raised me, who'd loved me unconditionally, who deserved to keep her home.

I just had to keep reminding myself of that. Had to keep the why clear in my mind, even as the how became increasingly complicated.

Even as some traitorous part of me started looking forward to the next call, the next command, the next time I'd kneel blindfolded on Samson's expensive rug and let him transform me into someone I barely recognized.

Someone who liked it.

I pushed the thought away and headed for the shower, needing to wash away the physical evidence of what I'd done even if I couldn't wash away the memory.

Two more days. Just two more days, and Grandma would be safe.

I could survive two more days.

Couldn't I?

CHAPTER 10

I couldn't stay home. If I stayed home, I'd just lie in bed replaying everything until I drove myself crazy. So despite my exhaustion, despite the fact that every movement reminded me of what I'd done, I got dressed for my evening shift at the hotel.

Work would be a distraction. Work would be normal. Work would remind me that I was still Madison Carter, hotel maid, not... whatever I'd been in that office.

The sun was setting as I pulled into the hotel parking lot, painting the sky in shades of orange and pink that I barely registered. My mind was elsewhere, caught in an endless loop of analysis and second-guessing.

Why hadn't Samson fucked me? That question haunted me more than it should have. He'd had the opportunity, had me positioned perfectly, had clearly wanted to. So why had he pulled away at the last moment? Why leave me desperate and aching instead of taking what he'd paid for?

Because this was about power, I reminded myself. About control. About showing me that he could have me whenever and however he wanted—or not at all, if that was his preference.

The realization should have made me angry. Instead, it made me shiver with a complicated mix of frustration and anticipation.

I clocked in and headed to the storage room to grab a cleaning cart, moving carefully to avoid aggravating the soreness in my lower back. The late shift was usually quieter, with fewer rooms to clean. Most guests checked in by three o'clock, so I'd only be servicing the rooms that hadn't been booked for the day—probably fifteen at most.

I could handle fifteen rooms. I could handle the monotonous routine of stripping beds and scrubbing toilets. I needed the mindlessness of it right now.

I was fitting fresh sheets onto the mattress in the first room when a knock on the door interrupted me. I looked up to see Josie leaning against the doorframe, her dark curls pulled back in a ponytail, her uniform slightly rumpled from a long shift at the front desk.

"Hey," she said, waving with a tired smile.

"Hey," I replied, finishing with the fitted sheet before standing up straight. The movement made my clothes rub against the welts on my ass, and I couldn't quite suppress the wince that followed.

Josie's eyebrows rose with concern. "You okay? You look like you're hurting."

"Just sore," I said quickly. "I, uh, took a bad fall on my bike the other day. Still healing."

It wasn't entirely a lie. I had fallen on my bike, even if that wasn't the source of my current discomfort.

"Ouch." Josie grimaced sympathetically. "Well, you're probably not going to like what I'm about to tell you then."

My stomach dropped. "What?"

"You won't believe who stopped by to see you earlier," she said, her voice taking on that conspiratorial tone she used when delivering gossip.

For one wild, irrational moment, my heart fluttered with possibility. Had Samson come looking for me? It had only been a few hours since I'd left his office, but maybe he'd realized he wanted more, wanted to actually fuck me instead of just teasing—

"Jason," Josie said, and the name landed like a bucket of cold water.

"What?" I stared at her, certain I'd misheard.

"Jason came by. Like, an hour ago. He was asking for you, said he needed to talk to you." Josie studied my face carefully. "I told him you weren't working until later, but I got the impression he might come back."

Disappointment washed over me in a wave so intense it was almost physical. Of course it hadn't been Samson. Why would it be? He'd gotten what he wanted from me today. He had two more days to claim whenever he felt like it. He certainly wouldn't waste his valuable time chasing after me at my job.

And why did that thought make me feel so hollow?

"Madison? You okay?" Josie's voice pulled me back to the present.

"Yeah. Sorry. Just... processing." I shook my head, trying to clear it. "What did he want?"

"He didn't say exactly, but..." Josie bit her lip. "I think he wants to apologize. For what he did. He looked pretty rough, honestly. Like he hasn't been sleeping."

"Good," I said flatly. "He should feel like shit."

"I know, I know." Josie held up her hands defensively. "But you two seemed so happy together before all this. Maybe it was just a moment of weakness? Everyone makes mistakes."

I felt anger kindle in my chest, hot and bright. "A mistake, Josie? Really? A mistake is forgetting to buy milk at the store. A mistake is sending a text to the wrong person. Cheating requires intent. He made a conscious choice to bring that woman into his bed—into the bed where I'd given him my virginity—and fuck her. That's not a mistake. That's a betrayal."

Josie looked taken aback by my vehemence. "You're right. I'm sorry. I didn't mean to minimize what he did."

I took a deep breath, forcing the anger back down. It wasn't fair to take this out on Josie. She was just trying to help in her own misguided way.

"I know you're trying to help," I said more gently. "But there's nothing Jason can say that will fix this. I don't want to see him, I don't want to talk to him, and if I never lay eyes on him again, that'll be perfectly fine with me."

"I understand." Josie gave me a sympathetic smile. "Well, I just thought you should know he came by. I'm off now, so I'm heading home. You need anything before I go?"

"No, I'm good. Thanks for the heads up."

"Anytime, girl. Hang in there."

She left, and I went back to making the bed with perhaps more force than necessary, yanking the top sheet into place and attacking the pillows with aggressive efficiency.

Jason. Of course he'd shown up now, when my life was already a complicated mess. Of course he wanted to apologize, probably expecting me to fall into his arms and forgive him because he said the magic words.

Well, fuck that. And fuck him.

I threw myself into the work with single-minded determination, cleaning room after room with meticulous care. Strip the bed. Check the bathroom. Vacuum the carpet. Dust the surfaces. Repeat. The routine was meditative, allowing my mind to finally quiet as my body went through the familiar motions.

By the time I'd finished all fifteen rooms, it was just past eleven. I still had an hour left on my shift, so I headed to the laundry room to start processing the mountain of towels and sheets that had accumulated.

The industrial washers and dryers hummed their rhythmic song as I sorted linens, and I found myself thinking about Samson again. About the contract sitting on my kitchen counter at home. About the two days I still owed him, and what those days might bring.

Would he whip me again? The thought made me clench involuntarily, my body remembering the sharp sting, the burning aftermath, the way pain had somehow transmuted into pleasure under his skilled manipulation.

Would he use his mouth on me again? The memory of his tongue in places no one had ever touched before sent heat pooling in my belly, made me shift uncomfortably on the hard plastic chair.

Would he finally fuck me?

That was the question that haunted me most. Why hadn't he? What was he waiting for? What did he want from me that I hadn't already given?

I was so lost in thought that I didn't notice how late it had gotten until the clock on the wall showed 11:50. Time to clock out.

I finished the load I'd been working on, returned the cleaning cart to storage, and headed to the time clock near the employee entrance. My body ached with exhaustion—the physical demands of the day with Samson followed by six hours of manual labor had left me wrung out and desperate for sleep.

The parking lot was mostly empty when I stepped outside, just a few employee vehicles scattered under the flickering lights. Half the lot lights were broken—had been for months—and management didn't seem inclined to fix them. I made a mental note to complain again, though I knew it wouldn't do any good.

My car was parked in the back corner, and as I walked toward it, I noticed a figure leaning against the trunk.

My hand immediately dove into my purse, fingers closing around the small canister of mace I kept for exactly this kind of situation. Working late hours in a poorly lit parking lot meant taking precautions. I slowed my steps, trying to make out details in the darkness.

The figure straightened and took a step toward me.

"Madison," a familiar voice called out, and my blood ran cold.

Jason.

"What do you want?" I demanded, my voice sharp enough to cut glass. I kept walking but didn't take my hand off the mace. "Josie said you came by earlier. I thought my lack of response would have been message enough."

"I needed to see you," he said, and even in the dim light, I could see he looked terrible. His hair was messy, his clothes wrinkled, his eyes red-rimmed and bloodshot. "I needed to apologize. To make this right."

"There is no making this right, Jason. We're done."

"Please, just hear me out—"

"I don't want to hear you out!" I snapped. "You cheated on me. You brought another woman into your bed—the bed where we slept together, where I gave you my virginity—and you fucked her. Then you had the audacity to still be hard when I walked in, like my presence was just an inconvenience."

He flinched at my words. "I know. I know it was terrible. I'm so sorry, Madison. I don't know what I was thinking."

"You were thinking with your dick, Jason. That's what you were thinking." I reached my car and moved to unlock it, but Jason stepped closer, forcing me to back against the driver's door.

"She didn't mean anything to me," he said desperately. "Lindsey was just... it was just sex. It meant nothing."

I laughed, the sound harsh and bitter. "Oh, let me guess. She left you, didn't she? That's why you're here now. Your convenient piece of ass moved on, and suddenly you remember I exist."

His silence was answer enough.

"Thank God I walked in on you," I continued, my voice dripping with sarcasm. "Otherwise I'd still be the idiot wasting my time on you, completely oblivious that my boyfriend was a lying, cheating piece of shit."

"You're not an idiot," Jason said quietly.

"I didn't say I was. But clearly you think I am if you believe I'm going to take you back after what you did."

"Madison, please." He reached for me, and I jerked away. "I love you. I miss you. We had something good together. Don't throw that away over one mistake."

"One mistake," I repeated, my voice dangerously calm. "There's that word again. Tell me, Jason—was it a mistake when you texted her? Was it a mistake when you invited her over? Was it a mistake when you kissed her? When you undressed her? When you got your dick hard for her? When you slid inside her?" My voice rose with each question until I was nearly shouting. "At what point exactly did this 'mistake' happen, Jason? Because from where I'm standing, you made about fifty conscious choices before your cock ended up in another woman."

He staggered back as if I'd physically struck him. "I don't know what you want me to say."

"I don't want you to say anything!" I moved to step around him, to get to my car door. "I want you to leave me alone. I want you to accept that we're over. I want you to go home and leave me the fuck alone."

"No." He moved to block me again, and I caught the scent of alcohol wafting off him in waves.

"Are you drunk?" I demanded, taking a step back. The smell was overpowering, making my eyes water. "Jesus, Jason, did you drive here like this?"

"I needed courage," he slurred slightly. "To come see you. To apologize properly."

"You need to leave," I said firmly. "You're drunk, and you're not thinking clearly. Go home. Sleep it off. And don't come back here."

I managed to get around him and reached for my car door handle, but Jason moved behind me, pressing close enough that I could feel the heat of his body. His hand slammed against the window above my head, caging me in.

"I'm not leaving without you," he said, his words running together. "I can't be without you, Madison. I love you. I fucking love you so much it hurts."

And God help me, the wall I'd built around my heart started to crack.

My eyes watered despite my best efforts to stop them. These were the words I'd wanted to hear two days ago, before everything fell apart. We'd been through so much together. Two years of my life invested in this relationship. Plans for the future. Talks about marriage and children and growing old together.

Could it really be over so suddenly? So completely?

I clenched my jaw and blinked furiously, forcing the tears back. Forcing the emotions down where they couldn't weaken my resolve.

Because he had fucked another woman. The image flashed through my mind with perfect clarity—that woman on her hands and knees, Jason behind her, his hands on her hips, his cock sliding in and out of her while she moaned. And then the way she'd smiled at me when she'd noticed me standing there. That cruel, satisfied smile that said she'd won something I hadn't even known was a competition.

The anger returned, flooding my senses like ice water, washing away the momentary weakness.

"GET THE FUCK AWAY FROM ME!" I screamed, whirling around and shoving Jason as hard as I could.

He staggered backward, his alcohol-impaired balance making him clumsy. For a moment, I thought he'd fall, but he managed to catch himself, arms windmilling for balance.

I yanked open my car door and threw myself inside, slamming it shut and immediately hitting the lock button. My hands shook as I fumbled for my keys, trying to get them into the ignition.

Jason stared at me through the window, his expression cycling rapidly through shock, hurt, and finally settling on rage. His face twisted into something ugly, something I'd never seen before.

"You bitch!" he shouted, and kicked the driver's side door hard enough to make the whole car shake.

I gasped, my hands shaking so badly I almost dropped the keys. The engine hesitated when I turned them, and pure panic flooded through me.

Not now. Please, not now. Start, you piece of shit, start!

Jason kicked the door again, and I heard something crack. He was screaming obscenities now, his fists pounding on the window, his face purple with drunken rage.

The engine caught. Held. Roared to life.

I threw the car into reverse and hit the gas, not caring that Jason was still standing close enough to be hit. He jumped back at the last second, still shouting, and I peeled out of the parking lot with my tires squealing against the asphalt.

My hands gripped the steering wheel so tightly my knuckles went white. My heart hammered against my ribs. My breath came in short, sharp gasps that sounded almost like sobs.

I'd seen Jason angry before—frustrated when things didn't go his way, irritated when I couldn't do something he wanted—but I'd never seen him like that. Never seen that kind of rage directed at me.

What would he have done if I hadn't gotten into the car? If the door hadn't been locked? If my car hadn't started?

The thoughts chased each other through my head as I drove home on autopilot, checking my rearview mirror compulsively to make sure he wasn't following me.

By the time I pulled into my driveway, my hands were still shaking and my throat was tight with suppressed emotion. I ran inside, locked the door behind me, and finally— finally—let myself break down.

I slid down the door to sit on the floor, pulled my knees to my chest, and burst into tears.

Great, heaving sobs tore through me, weeks of stress and heartbreak and confusion and fear pouring out all at once. I cried for the relationship I'd lost. I cried for the man I'd thought Jason was. I cried for my grandmother and her house. I cried for the choices I'd made and the person I was becoming.

I cried until there was nothing left, until my throat was raw and my eyes were swollen and I felt hollowed out and empty.

And then, when the tears finally stopped, I dragged myself off the floor and stumbled to my bedroom. I didn't bother changing out of my work clothes. I just collapsed onto my bed and stared at the ceiling, my mind blessedly numb.

My phone buzzed on the nightstand. A text message.

For one horrible moment, I thought it might be Jason, and my stomach clenched with anxiety. But when I checked, it was from an unknown number.

I hope your evening was satisfactory. Rest well. You'll need your strength for our next encounter. - SL

Samson.

I stared at the message for a long moment, my thumb hovering over the reply button. A thousand responses ran through my mind—

questions about when he'd call next, about what he'd want from me, about why he hadn't fucked me today.

In the end, I just typed: *Yes, sir*.

His response came almost immediately: *Good girl*.

Those two words sent a shiver through my exhausted body and chased away some of the hollow feeling Jason's appearance had left behind.

I set the phone aside and closed my eyes, and despite everything—despite the confrontation with Jason, despite the soreness in my body, despite the impossible situation I'd gotten myself into—I fell asleep almost immediately.

And when I dreamed, it wasn't of Jason's rage or that woman's cruel smile.

It was of dark eyes and commanding voices and hands that could hurt and heal in equal measure.

It was of the Wolf, and the two days I still owed him.

And God help me, I couldn't wait.

CHAPTER 11

I woke up freezing.

The cold had seeped into my bones overnight, turning my bedroom into something resembling a meat locker. I could see my breath misting in the air above me, and when I reluctantly stuck a hand out from under the covers to check my phone, my fingers immediately went numb.

I stayed bundled under the covers for a long time, cocooned in the warmth I'd built up overnight, not wanting to face the day or the cold or the complicated mess my life had become.

But eventually, hunger won out over comfort.

I forced myself out of bed and immediately regretted it as the frigid air hit my skin. I grabbed a sweatshirt from the floor—probably dirty, but I didn't care—and pulled it on over my pajamas before padding into the kitchen.

The kitchen felt even colder than my bedroom, if that was possible. I made toast and instant coffee because they required minimal exposure to the icy air, eating standing up at the counter while mentally calculating whether I could afford to get the heat fixed this month.

Probably not. Not if I wanted to eat. The eternal struggle of being poor—deciding which basic necessity to sacrifice this week.

After breakfast, I forced myself to take another shower, hoping the hot water would help ease the soreness in my muscles and maybe warm me up enough to face the day.

The water came out ice cold.

I stood there staring at the showerhead in disbelief, turning the hot water knob all the way up and getting nothing but arctic spray for my efforts.

"You've got to be fucking kidding me," I muttered, turning the water off and wrapping my arms around myself.

The water heater had died. Of course it had. Because why would anything in my life work properly?

I did the mental math quickly and came to the depressing conclusion that my next paycheck would have to go toward fixing the water heater. Winter was coming, and as much as I needed my car to be reliable, I needed hot water more. I could walk to work if I had to—the town wasn't that big, and I'd walked farther for less important reasons.

But I couldn't survive a winter without hot water. Not in this climate.

I dressed in layers, trying to generate some body heat, and I was exhausted again despite having just woken up a few hours ago. I collapsed onto the couch and stared blankly at the ceiling, trying not to think about anything at all.

The soreness in my ass was still present, but less intense than yesterday. I twisted awkwardly to check myself in the mirror hanging on the wall, pulling down my sweatpants enough to see the damage.

The red marks were still visible, faded to pink now but definitely still there. Light bruising had formed around the edges where Samson had struck me repeatedly. I traced one of the marks with my finger, and the touch sent a confusing mix of discomfort and arousal through me.

Hopefully, whatever Samson had planned for the next session would be less focused on pain and more on pleasure. Though even as I thought it, I wasn't entirely sure I meant it. There had been something about the pain—the way it built and faded, the way it sharpened my awareness of my own body, the way it somehow made the pleasure that followed more intense.

I still couldn't wrap my head around why he hadn't fucked me. Maybe he was saving it for the last day? Building anticipation? Playing some kind of psychological game where denying me what I wanted would make me more desperate when he finally gave it to me?

Whatever his reasoning, it was working. I couldn't stop thinking about what it would feel like to have him inside me, couldn't stop imagining his body pressing mine into that soft rug, his voice in my ear telling me I was a good girl while he—

My phone rang, startling me out of my increasingly explicit fantasy.

I grabbed it from the coffee table and swiped to answer without looking at the caller ID, still half-lost in thoughts of Samson.

"Hello?"

"Madison." His voice sent electricity down my spine, like I'd somehow summoned him with my thoughts.

I sat up immediately, suddenly wide awake. "Samson. Hi."

"I trust you're not too sore from yesterday?" There was amusement in his tone, like he knew exactly how sore I was and was enjoying it.

"No, of course not," I lied smoothly. "I'm fine."

"Good. Because I want to see you today."

My heart rate kicked up several notches. "Today? I thought—I mean, don't you need more time between..." I trailed off, not sure how to phrase it.

"Between what? Sessions?" He sounded even more amused now. "Madison, I have six months to claim my three days. I can space them out however I please. And today, I'm pleased to see you again."

"Okay," I said, trying to sound calm and collected despite the way my pulse was racing. "What time? Should I come to your office?"

"No. I'll be picking you up at your house. Be ready at five-thirty. And Madison?"

"Yes?"

"Wear something nice. A dress, preferably. Something short that shows off those beautiful legs of yours."

I blinked in surprise, my mind struggling to reconcile this instruction with what I'd expected. "A dress?"

"Yes. Is that a problem?"

"No, I just—" I hesitated, then decided to push a little. "Is there anything specific you want me to wear under the dress?"

His low chuckle sent heat pooling in my belly. "Surprise me. I do enjoy a good surprise."

"Okay. I'll be ready."

"See that you are. I don't like to be kept waiting." There was a pause, and then his voice dropped lower, became more intimate. "I'm looking forward to seeing you, Madison. To continuing what we started yesterday."

"Me too," I whispered, and realized with a start that I meant it.

"Five-thirty sharp."

He hung up without waiting for a response, leaving me sitting on my couch with my phone pressed to my ear and my mind racing.

He wanted me to dress nice. To wear a dress. A short dress.

Was he taking me somewhere? The thought sent my imagination into overdrive. Dinner, maybe? There was an upscale restaurant Samson favored—Rossini's, an Italian place downtown where a single entrée cost more than I spent on groceries in a week. I'd been there once, years ago, when my mother was still married to him. I'd felt completely out of place the entire evening, surrounded by people in designer clothes discussing wine vintages and vacation homes.

Was this... a date?

The thought was absurd. We had a contract. This was a business arrangement, a transactional relationship where I provided sexual services in exchange for debt forgiveness. You didn't take someone on a date when you were paying them for sex.

But then why the dress code? Why pick me up instead of having me come to his office? Why the emphasis on looking nice?

I stood up and started pacing, my mind churning through possibilities. Maybe this was part of his plan—wine and dine me, make me feel special, lower my defenses before he did whatever he had planned for today. It was a manipulation tactic, clearly, designed to make me more compliant, more willing to do whatever he asked.

The problem was, it was already working.

I couldn't deny that my feelings toward Samson were becoming... complicated. Before all this started, I'd barely thought about him. He was my mother's ex-husband, a successful businessman with a ruthless reputation, someone who existed at the periphery of my life but never really touched it.

Now? I couldn't get him out of my head.

His voice, his touch, the way he looked at me like I was something precious and disposable at the same time. The way he could make me feel powerful and helpless with just a few words. The way my body responded to him despite every logical reason it shouldn't.

"Keep a clear mind," I muttered to myself, but the words rang hollow.

My mind was anything but clear where Samson Lang was concerned.

I checked the time on my phone—11:47 AM. I had less than six hours to find a dress, make myself look presentable, and mentally prepare for whatever Samson had planned.

First problem: I didn't own a short dress.

I went to my bedroom and started digging through my closet with increasing desperation. I had exactly one dress, purchased for senior prom and never worn since. I pulled it out of the plastic garment bag it had been stored in and held it up critically.

It was floor-length and flowing, a soft blue color that had seemed sophisticated and grown-up when I was eighteen. Now it just looked dated and completely wrong for what Samson had requested.

I tried it on anyway, hoping maybe it would work, but the moment I pulled it over my head, I knew it was hopeless. It was too tight across the chest—apparently I'd developed a bit more since high school—and even if I could have squeezed into it, it was the opposite of short.

I threw it on the bed in frustration and continued searching through my limited wardrobe. Work clothes. Jeans. T-shirts. A few sweaters. Nothing even remotely close to what Marcus had requested.

I stood there staring at the meager contents of my closet and felt panic starting to set in. I couldn't show up in jeans and a t-shirt, not when he'd specifically asked for a dress. But I also couldn't afford to buy one—my bank account was running on fumes until my next paycheck, and that was still days away.

Which meant I needed to borrow one.

I mentally ran through the list of people I could ask. My options were extremely limited. I didn't have many friends—working and caring for my grandmother didn't leave much time for a social life—and the few I had weren't exactly dress-wearing types.

Except Josie.

Josie, who loved fashion and always looked put-together even in the hotel's drab uniform.

Josie, who was about my size and had mentioned more than once that she had a closet full of clothes she never wore.

I grabbed my phone and sent her a text before I could second-guess myself: *Hey, random question—do you have a short dress I could borrow? Like, cocktail length or shorter?*

Her response came back almost immediately: *OMG yes! I have like 10. What's the occasion?*

Long story. Can I see pics?

A series of photos started coming through, each one showing a different dress. Some were too formal, some too casual, some just not my style. But the fifth one made me stop scrolling.

It was perfect.

Black, fitted but not too tight, with a sweetheart neckline and a hem that would hit mid-thigh. Elegant but with a hint of sexiness. Exactly the kind of dress Marcus would appreciate.

Before I could even type out a request, my phone rang. Josie.

"Hey," I answered.

"Hey yourself. So you need a dress. What's this about? Hot date?"

"Sort of. It's... complicated."

"Complicated how?" I could hear the curiosity in her voice. "Please tell me you're not getting back together with Jason."

"God, no. Absolutely not. This is... someone else."

"Someone else?" Josie's tone shifted to excited. "Madison Carter, are you seeing someone new? Already? It's been like three days!"

"It's not like that. It's—" I fumbled for an explanation that wouldn't be a complete lie. "It's a business dinner. Kind of. A professional meeting, but at a nice restaurant, so I need to look the part."

"A professional meeting where you need to look hot?" Josie sounded skeptical but amused. "Okay, sure. I'm not judging. Which dress did you like?"

"The black one. The fifth picture you sent."

"Oh, that's a good choice. That one looks amazing on—you know what, it'll look amazing on you. Makes your legs look incredible. Very sexy but still classy."

"Perfect. Can I borrow it?"

"Of course. But I have one condition."

My stomach dropped. "What?"

"I get to do your hair and makeup."

"Josie, I don't need—"

"Yes, you absolutely do," she interrupted firmly. "If you're going to wear my dress, you're going to wear it right. Full glamour. Hair, makeup, the works. I have the day off, and honestly, I would love an excuse to play dress-up with someone who isn't me. Please?"

I hesitated, but only for a second. The truth was, I had no idea how to do makeup beyond the basics, and my hair styling skills consisted of "ponytail" and "messy bun." If I was going to do this, I might as well do it right.

"Okay. Thank you. When can you come over?"

"Give me an hour. I need to grab some supplies. This is going to be so fun!"

She hung up before I could respond, leaving me standing in my bedroom surrounded by rejected clothing and wondering what I'd just gotten myself into.

True to her word, Josie showed up at my door an hour later with a massive bag full of makeup and hair products, the dress draped carefully over her arm.

"Okay," she said, sweeping into my freezing apartment without waiting for an invitation. "First question: Jesus Christ, why is it so cold in here? Second question: what time do you need to be ready by?"

"Heat's broken. Water heater too, actually. And I need to be ready by five-thirty."

Josie's eyes widened. "Girl. You're living in an icebox with no hot water? Why didn't you tell me?"

I shrugged, embarrassed. "It just happened. I'll get it fixed when I get paid."

"That's... that's not okay. You know what, we'll talk about this later. Right now, we have a transformation to accomplish." She checked her watch. "It's one o'clock. That gives us four and a half hours. Perfect. Strip."

"What?"

"Strip. I need to see what we're working with. Body type, skin tone, all of it. Then we'll do hair and makeup, and you'll get dressed last so nothing gets messed up. Come on, chop chop."

I'd forgotten how aggressively enthusiastic Josie could be when she got excited about something. I did as instructed, stripping down to my underwear while trying not to feel self-conscious.

Josie circled me like a fashion designer evaluating a mannequin, nodding thoughtfully. "Okay. Good bone structure, nice curves, skin's a little dry but we can work with that. Turn around."

I turned, and heard her sharp intake of breath.

"Madison. What the hell happened to your back?"

Shit. I'd forgotten about the marks Samson had left.

"I, uh—" My mind raced for a plausible explanation. "I fell. Off my bike, remember? I told you about that."

"That does not look like bike injuries. Those look like—" She paused, and when she spoke again, her voice was carefully neutral. "Those look like marks from something else."

Heat flooded my face. "It's nothing. They don't hurt anymore."

Josie was quiet for a long moment, and I could feel her studying me, putting pieces together. When she finally spoke, her voice was gentle.

"This business dinner. Is it really a business dinner?"

"Yes," I said firmly, turning to face her. "It is. I'm not—it's complicated, okay? But I'm not in danger or doing anything I don't want to do. I promise."

She searched my face, then nodded slowly. "Okay. I believe you. But Madison? If you ever need help, or need to talk, or need a place to crash—"

"I know. Thank you."

"All right." She clapped her hands together, breaking the serious moment. "Enough heavy stuff. Let's make you look so hot that whoever this is falls over themselves trying to impress you."

The next four hours passed in a blur of activity.

Josie worked with the focused intensity of a surgeon, starting with my skin. She exfoliated, moisturized, primed, and then began the careful work of applying foundation that somehow made my skin look flawless while still looking like skin.

"The key," she explained as she worked, "is to enhance what you have, not cover it up. You want to look like a better version of yourself, not like you're wearing a mask."

Contouring followed, then blush, then highlighter applied with such precision I was afraid to move. My eyes were next—a smoky look that made them seem bigger and more dramatic, with long lashes that were definitely not my own.

"These are strip lashes," Josie explained as she carefully applied glue. "They'll feel weird at first, but they make such a difference. Just don't rub your eyes."

Finally, lipstick—a deep red that I never would have chosen for myself but that somehow looked perfect once it was on.

"There," Josie said with satisfaction, turning me to face the mirror. "Phase one complete."

I stared at my reflection and barely recognized myself. My skin looked luminous.

My eyes looked huge and mysterious. My lips looked full and pouty in a way I'd never achieved on my own.

"Holy shit," I whispered.

"Right? And we're not done yet. Hair time."

The hair process was even more involved. Josie washed it first—complaining the entire time about my cold water situation—then blow-dried and curled it section by section, creating loose waves that tumbled over my shoulders. She pinned back one side with bobby pins, creating an asymmetrical look that was elegant and slightly edgy at the same time.

"Hairspray," she commanded, and I closed my eyes while she shellacked the whole thing in place.

When she was finally done, it was 5:15.

"Dress time," she announced. "Carefully. Don't mess up the hair or makeup."

I stepped into the dress while Josie held it steady, then she zipped up the back and adjusted the neckline.

"Shoes?"

"I only have these." I showed her my single pair of black heels, purchased years ago for a job interview and rarely worn since.

"Those'll work. Put them on. And here—" She pulled out a small black clutch from her seemingly bottomless bag. "You can borrow this too. It goes better with the dress than your normal purse."

I slipped on the heels and took the clutch, transferring my phone, ID, and keys into it.

"Okay," Josie said, stepping back to survey her work. "Turn around. Slowly."

I did a slow spin.

"Holy shit, Madison." Josie's eyes were wide. "You look incredible. Like, seriously. I knew you were pretty, but damn. You clean up nice."

I looked at myself in the full-length mirror and felt my breath catch.

The woman looking back at me was a stranger. Sophisticated. Sexy. Confident. The kind of woman who could walk into a fancy restaurant on Samson's arm and not look out of place.

For the first time in a long while, I felt beautiful.

"Thank you," I said softly. "Really. I don't know what I would have done without you."

"That's what friends are for." Josie checked her watch. "It's 5:28. I should get out of here so you can make your grand entrance. But seriously—text me later and tell me how it goes. I'm dying to know what this is really about."

"I will. I promise."

She gathered up her supplies and headed for the door, then paused and turned back.

"Madison? Whoever this person is? They're lucky to have your time. Don't forget that."

She left before I could respond, and I stood alone in my freezing apartment, dressed like I was going to a ball, waiting for a man who'd paid for the privilege of my company.

At exactly 5:30, I heard a car pull into my driveway.

I peeked through the curtains and saw a sleek black Town Car—not Marcus's Mercedes, something even more elegant. A driver in a crisp suit got out and started walking toward my door.

My heart hammered in my chest. This was really happening.

I grabbed the clutch, took one final look in the mirror, and stepped outside.

The driver smiled politely and offered his arm. "Ms. Carter? Mr. Lang is waiting."

I took his arm and let him guide me to the car, my heels clicking against the concrete of my driveway. He opened the rear door with practiced grace, and I slid inside.

Samson was sitting in the seat beside me, dressed in a perfectly tailored charcoal suit that probably cost more than my car. His dark hair was styled with just enough product to look effortless, his jaw freshly shaved, and when he turned to look at me, I saw his expression transform.

For just a moment—so quick I almost missed it—his carefully controlled mask slipped, and I saw genuine surprise and admiration flash across his face.

"You look stunning," he said softly, his voice carrying a note I'd never heard before. Awe, almost.

"Thank you," I replied, looking out the window so he wouldn't see how much his reaction pleased me.

I caught his reflection in the glass and saw him smile—not his usual calculating smirk, but something warmer, more genuine.

The driver closed my door and got behind the wheel, and as we pulled out of my driveway, I felt Samson's eyes still on me, studying me like I was a puzzle he was just beginning to solve.

"Where are we going?" I asked, finally turning to meet his gaze.

His smile widened, gaining that predatory edge I was becoming familiar with.

"Somewhere we can talk," he said. "And get to know each other better. After all, we have all evening, and I intend to make the most of it."

The car glided smoothly onto the main road, and I realized that I wasn't nervous. I was excited.

CHAPTER 12

I'd been right about the destination.

The car pulled into the parking lot of Rossini's, and even in the fading evening light, the restaurant looked exactly as I remembered it—imposing, elegant, and completely out of my league.

The exterior was designed to evoke a rustic Italian villa, all warm stone and weathered wood that had probably been artfully distressed by expensive craftsmen. A large wrought-iron sign hung over the entrance, featuring an ornate fish skeleton worked into an intricate design that probably had some symbolic meaning I didn't understand. The doorway was framed by pillars carved to resemble classical columns, the kind of architectural detail that screamed old money and sophisticated taste.

My mouth watered involuntarily at the memory of the food they served here. I'd skipped lunch entirely to ensure I'd have room for dinner—a decision born partly from practicality and partly from the fact that my refrigerator was currently home to half a jar of grape jelly and some questionable leftovers. But now, with my stomach completely empty and the scent of expensive Italian cooking wafting through the car's air vents, I was regretting not at least grabbing a snack.

The driver smoothly exited the vehicle and came around to my door, opening it with practiced efficiency. He extended his hand to help me out—a gentlemanly gesture I wasn't used to—and I accepted it gratefully, careful not to catch my heels on the car's interior.

The cool evening air hit my bare legs, making me shiver slightly. Samson's door opened, and I watched as he stepped out with that effortless grace that seemed to come naturally to him, like even the simple act of exiting a vehicle was something he'd perfected through years of practice.

He was devastating in his formal attire.

The suit was all black, clearly bespoke, tailored so perfectly it looked like it had been painted onto his body. Silver buttons glinted at the cuffs and down the front of his jacket, catching the light from the restaurant's exterior lamps. His tie was a rich navy blue that somehow made his dark eyes look even more intense, and his shirt was such a crisp, vivid white that it practically glowed.

I tried to think of a time when I'd seen Samson dressed casually—jeans and a t-shirt, sweats, anything normal—but in every memory I had, he was always like this. Polished. Perfect. Powerful.

He came around to my side of the car and extended his arm in invitation. I slipped my hand into the crook of his elbow, and we walked toward the restaurant entrance together, our hands clasped like we were an actual couple on an actual date.

The thought sent a confusing flutter through my chest.

This wasn't a date. This was... what? Part of our arrangement? Another form of payment extraction? I still wasn't entirely sure why Samson had chosen to take me out to dinner instead of just using me in his office again, but I'd already decided I was going to enjoy it regardless.

When would I ever get another chance to eat at a place like this?

The moment we stepped through the doors, I was enveloped in warmth and the heavenly scent of garlic, wine, and slow-cooked tomato sauce. The interior was even more elegant than I remembered—all dark wood and soft lighting, with white tablecloths and crystal wine glasses.

A host in a sleek black suit approached us immediately, his professional smile widening when he saw Samson.

"Mr. Lang, welcome back. Your table is ready."

Of course Samson had made reservations. Of course he was recognized on sight. I wondered how often he came here, whether this was his regular spot for impressing business associates or entertaining... whatever I was.

"Thank you, David," Samson replied smoothly, and the casual use of the host's name suggested this was indeed a regular haunt.

As David gathered menus and began explaining something about the night's specials, I let my gaze wander around the restaurant, taking in details I'd been too young to appreciate on my previous visit.

The place was packed. Every table was occupied by well-dressed diners engaged in quiet conversation, their jewelry catching the candlelight, their laughter refined and cultured. I recognized a few faces—the mayor was at a corner table with what looked like his family, and I was pretty sure that couple near the window owned half the commercial real estate in town.

These were Samson's people. The wealthy elite of Brookhaven, the ones who made decisions in boardrooms and country clubs while people like me scrubbed their hotel toilets.

"Madison." Samson's voice pulled my attention away from a particularly striking painting on the wall—something abstract and expensive-looking. He was watching me with amusement, his hand extended again. "Shall we?"

I took his hand and let him guide me through the crowded restaurant, acutely aware of the eyes that followed our progress. People were looking at us—at him, certainly, because Samson Lang commanded attention wherever he went, but also at me. The unknown woman on his arm, dressed in borrowed finery, trying desperately to look like I belonged here.

Our table was in a semi-private alcove near the back, slightly separated from the main dining area by a decorative screen. It was intimate without being completely isolated—we could see the restaurant, but we also had a sense of privacy that the other diners lacked.

Samson pulled out my chair before the host could, and I sat down carefully, hyperaware of the short hem of my dress and the way it rode up my thighs. When I looked up, I caught Samson's eyes tracking the movement, a flicker of heat in his gaze before his professional mask reasserted itself.

"Order anything you want," he said once we were both seated and the host had departed with promises that our server would be right with us. "Don't be frugal. Don't look at the prices. Just order what sounds good."

I picked up the leather-bound menu with hands that weren't quite steady and opened it.

My eyes immediately went to the prices listed in elegant script beside each dish, and I had to suppress a gasp.

The appetizers alone were more than I spent on groceries in a week. A simple salad cost twenty-eight dollars. The pasta dishes started at forty-five. And the steaks—my mouth watered just reading the descriptions—ranged from sixty to over a hundred dollars for the premium cuts.

A hundred dollars. For one piece of meat.

I could feed myself for two weeks on that.

"I said don't look at the prices," Samson chided gently, and I realized he'd been watching my reaction. "This is my treat, Madison. Indulge yourself."

"I've never..." I trailed off, not sure how to finish that sentence without sounding pathetic. I'd never spent this much on a single meal? I'd never been anywhere this nice? I'd never felt so completely out of my depth?

"I know," he said simply, and there was understanding in his voice rather than judgment. "That's part of why I brought you here. I want you to experience things you couldn't afford on your own. Consider it one of the perks of our arrangement."

Our arrangement. Right. Because this wasn't a date, wasn't romance, wasn't anything except another form of the transaction we'd agreed to.

I focused on the menu, trying to ignore the complicated knot of emotions in my chest. My stomach growled audibly, as if reminding me that philosophy could wait but hunger couldn't.

The steak section drew my eye again. I'd always loved a good steak, but it was a luxury I rarely afforded myself. The descriptions were mouthwatering—dry-aged ribeye, filet mignon with truffle butter, New York strip with peppercorn crust.

I decided on the filet, medium-rare, with garlic mashed potatoes and roasted vegetables. If Samson wanted me to indulge, I might as well do it properly.

Our server arrived—a woman in her thirties with her dark hair pulled back in an elegant chignon, her uniform impeccable. She introduced herself as Mindy and took our drink orders first. Samson requested a specific wine, rattling off a year and vineyard that meant nothing to me but made Mindy's eyes light up with appreciation.

"Excellent choice, Mr. Lang. That's one of our finest vintages."

Of course it was.

We placed our food orders, and Mindy departed with promises to return with the wine momentarily. I settled back in my chair and found Samson watching me again, that intense gaze that seemed to see right through all my carefully constructed defenses.

"What is it?" he asked, though he hadn't looked away from his phone, which he'd pulled out to check.

I smiled slightly, impressed that he'd noticed my attention even while apparently distracted. "I was just trying to figure out why you brought me here."

Samson put his phone away and gave me his full attention. The shift was immediate and complete—one moment he was the busy businessman checking emails, the next he was entirely focused on me with an intensity that made my breath catch.

"I'm not a monster," he said quietly. "Despite what you may have thought when we first made our arrangement."

"I never said you were a monster."

"No, but you thought it." His lips quirked in a slight smile. "Don't bother denying it. I could see it in your eyes that day in my office. You thought I was heartless, cruel, taking advantage of your desperation."

I wanted to protest, but he wasn't wrong.

"If I'm going to have my way with you," Samson continued, his voice dropping lower, "it's going to be in every way that I want. There are times when I crave what we did yesterday—when I want to push you, test your limits, watch you submit to me completely."

Heat flooded through me at the memory, and from the knowing look in his eyes, he could tell.

"But there are also times," he said, "when I want the company of a lady. When I want intelligent conversation over good food, when I want to look across the table at someone beautiful and engaging. When I want to enjoy all the... other aspects of companionship."

"You called me a lady," I said softly, surprised by how much the word affected me.

"Aren't you?" He tilted his head slightly, studying me. "You've shown more grace and dignity in impossible circumstances than most people show in their entire lives. You're putting yourself through something you find degrading to save your grandmother. That takes strength, Madison. It takes character. Those are the qualities of a lady, not a—"

He cut himself off, but I knew what he'd been about to say. Not a whore. Not a slut. Not any of the degrading terms he'd used yesterday while I was on my knees for him.

The contrast was jarring and oddly touching.

"I remember being in this restaurant before," I said, changing the subject before the moment could become too heavy. "But it feels different somehow. I don't know if that makes any sense."

"Perfect sense," Samson replied. "This place hasn't changed—not in any significant way. The menu's evolved slightly, they've updated some of the décor, but fundamentally it's the same restaurant you visited years ago. What's changed is you. Your circumstances. Your perspective."

"My relationship to you," I added quietly.

"Yes. That too." He leaned back as Mindy returned with the wine, performing the ritual of presenting the bottle and pouring a small amount for Samson to taste.

He swirled it, sniffed it, sipped it, and nodded his approval. Elena poured for both of us—a generous amount that probably cost more than I wanted to think about—and departed again.

I took a sip and had to suppress a sound of pleasure. It was incredible—smooth and complex with flavors I couldn't even begin to identify. Nothing like the cheap wine I occasionally bought for cooking.

"Good?" Samson asked, amusement dancing in his eyes.

"I don't know enough about wine to say anything intelligent," I admitted. "But yes. It's delicious."

"That's the only review that matters."

We fell into comfortable conversation then, carefully avoiding any mention of our arrangement or what had happened yesterday or what might happen later tonight. Instead, we talked about innocuous things—books we'd read, places we'd traveled (or in my case, places I wanted to travel), opinions on movies and music.

I learned that Samson had a surprising love of classic literature, that he'd been to Italy three times and spoke passable Italian, that he played piano though he hadn't touched a keyboard in years.

He learned that I'd wanted to be a teacher before financial reality had forced me into hotel work, that I'd never been outside the state, that I had a secret addiction to true crime podcasts that I listened to while cleaning rooms.

It was... nice. Disturbingly nice. Like we were actually two people getting to know each other, rather than a powerful man and the woman he'd essentially bought.

Our food arrived, and my first bite of the filet made me actually moan—a soft sound I tried to suppress but failed. The meat was so tender it practically melted on my tongue, seasoned perfectly, cooked exactly to my specifications.

"Good?" Samson asked again, and this time there was definitely heat in his gaze.

"Incredible," I managed. "I've never had anything like this."

"There's a lot you've never had," he said quietly. "A lot I'd like to give you."

The words hung in the air between us, laden with meaning that went well beyond food.

We ate in companionable silence for a while, and I found myself studying him when I thought he wasn't looking. The strong line of his jaw. The way his hair fell slightly across his forehead. The elegant movements of his hands as he cut his steak.

He was handsome. I'd always known that objectively, but seeing him like this—relaxed, smiling, the harsh businessman persona softened by wine and good food—he was almost unbearably attractive.

And that attraction was getting harder and harder to deny or dismiss as just physical response to someone who held power over me.

"Dessert?" Mindy asked when she returned to clear our plates.

I wanted to say yes. God, I wanted to try one of their famous desserts—I'd heard people rave about their tiramisu. But I was comfortably full, and the idea of eating more seemed excessive.

"I shouldn't," I said reluctantly. "I'm completely stuffed."

"We'll take the tiramisu to go," Samson told Mindy smoothly. "Two forks."

She nodded and departed, and I raised an eyebrow at him.

"To go?"

"For later," he said, his voice dropping into that darker register that sent shivers through me. "After we work up an appetite again."

Oh.

Heat flooded through me, pooling low in my belly. So tonight wasn't over. I'd suspected as much, but having it confirmed made my pulse quicken.

I shifted in my seat and realized with surprise that the soreness from yesterday was almost completely gone. The welts had faded, and the ache in my muscles had subsided. My body had healed faster than I'd expected.

Ready for whatever Samson had planned next.

I leaned forward across the table, deliberately letting the neckline of my dress dip lower. I saw Samson's eyes flick down, tracking the movement, lingering on the swell of my breasts before returning to my face.

"So," I said softly, "you've got one day left after this. Any plans on how you intend to use it?"

"I prefer to live in the moment," Samson replied, matching my quiet tone. "And this day isn't over yet."

"That's true." I let a slow smile curve my lips. "What did you have in mind?"

Samson leaned forward as well, closing the distance between us until our faces were only inches apart. His eyes flicked past me, scanning the restaurant, then returned to hold my gaze with an intensity that made my breath catch.

"Go to the restroom," he whispered. "I'll meet you there in a moment."

My heart kicked into overdrive. "What for?"

The fire that blazed in his eyes was answer enough, but he said it anyway, his voice rough with desire:

"I have a craving."

CHAPTER 13

I stood at the sink in the ladies' room, pretending to fix my makeup while my heart hammered against my ribs.

Another woman was in here with me—an older lady in pearls and an expensive-looking dress, touching up her own lipstick. I willed her to leave, silently pleading with the universe to give me privacy before Samson arrived.

Because he was coming. I knew it with absolute certainty. The heat in his eyes when he'd told me to come here, the rough edge to his voice—this wasn't a suggestion to powder my nose. This was a command, and I was going to obey it.

The realization sent a complicated mix of anticipation and anxiety through my system.

I stared at my reflection in the ornate mirror, seeing a woman I barely recognized. The makeup Josie had applied was still perfect, my lips still that deep red that made them look fuller and more sensual. My hair fell in artful waves over my shoulders. I looked sophisticated, elegant, like the kind of woman who belonged in a place like this.

But underneath the surface, I could feel the truth worming its way into my consciousness, impossible to ignore any longer.

I was enjoying this. Not just tolerating it, not just enduring it for my grandmother's sake—actually, genuinely enjoying it.

I was enjoying Samson. His attention, his dominance, the way he looked at me like I was something precious and wicked at the same time. What had started as a desperate bargain to save Grandma's house was becoming something else entirely. Something more complex, more dangerous.

Something that felt disturbingly like desire.

The thought should have terrified me. Should have sent me running from this bathroom, from the restaurant, from Samson and his dark eyes and commanding voice. Instead, it made my pulse quicken with anticipation for what was about to happen.

The woman beside me finished with her lipstick and snapped her compact shut with a decisive click. She caught my eye in the mirror and smiled—a polite, distant smile that wealthy women seemed to perfect—before heading toward the door.

"Have a lovely evening, dear," she said as she passed.

"You too," I managed, my voice steadier than I felt.

The door swung shut behind her with a soft whoosh, leaving me alone in the bathroom. I turned to face the door and waited, my hands gripping the edge of the marble counter behind me.

Seconds ticked by. My breathing seemed unnaturally loud in the quiet space. I could hear muffled conversation and clinking silverware from the restaurant beyond, but in here, it felt like a pocket universe—separate, isolated.

The door opened.

Samson stepped inside with the casual confidence of a man who'd never questioned his right to be anywhere he wanted. He waited for the door to close, then reached behind him and flicked the lock with a soft click that seemed to echo through the bathroom.

Then he turned his full attention to me, and the intensity in his gaze nearly knocked me backward.

His eyes traveled over me slowly, deliberately—from my face down to my heels and back up again, lingering on my legs, my hips, the swell of my breasts visible above the neckline of the dress. It wasn't the polite appreciation of earlier. This was raw hunger, barely restrained desire, and it sent shivers cascading down my spine.

My pussy clenched involuntarily, already responding to just the way he was looking at me.

We locked eyes across the bathroom, and something passed between us—some unspoken understanding, some shift in the dynamic that had been building all evening.

My legs moved of their own volition.

I crossed the space between us in three quick steps and threw myself at him with an abandon that would have shocked me if I'd stopped to think about it. But I wasn't thinking anymore. I was just feeling, just wanting, just needing with an intensity that bordered on desperation.

Samson caught me easily, his arms wrapping around me and pulling me flush against his body. His mouth crashed down on mine, and I opened for him immediately, my tongue meeting his in a kiss that was anything but gentle.

This wasn't the careful, controlled Marcus from dinner. This was something primal and raw, and it ignited something equally wild in me.

I ran my hands over his chest, feeling the hard planes of muscle beneath his expensive shirt, then up to his neck where I could feel his pulse pounding as hard as mine. My fingers twisted into his hair, probably messing up his perfect styling, and I didn't care. I just needed to touch him, to pull him closer, to—

Samson pushed me backward until my ass hit the counter. Without breaking the kiss, he gripped my waist and lifted me onto the marble surface in one smooth motion. I wrapped my legs around him automatically, using them to pull him even closer.

His hand slid under my dress, skating up my thigh with deliberate slowness that made me whimper against his mouth. Higher, higher, until his fingers brushed against my lace-covered mound and I moaned softly into the kiss.

He pulled back just enough to look at me, his eyes dark with desire, his breathing as ragged as mine.

"So responsive," he murmured, his fingers tracing the edge of my panties. "Do you have any idea how fucking beautiful you are like this? Desperate for my touch?"

I couldn't form words. Could only nod and rock my hips forward, seeking more contact.

Samson's fingers slipped beneath the lace, and I gasped at the first skin-to-skin contact. He was so warm, his touch both gentle and firm as he explored my pussy.

"Already soaking for me," he said, approval rich in his voice. "Such a good girl."

Those words—*good girl*—sent a bolt of pleasure straight through me. I parted my legs wider in silent invitation, offering myself more completely.

His fingers rubbed between my labia with maddening expertise, finding all the sensitive spots that made my breath hitch and my hips jerk. He circled my entrance but didn't push inside, just teased with the promise of penetration while his thumb found my clit and pressed against it with perfect pressure.

I reached down to his waist, my hands fumbling with his belt buckle before finding the bulge straining against his pants. Even through the fabric, I could feel how hard he was, how much he wanted this. I rubbed my palm against his length, and Samson groaned—a low, rough sound that made me feel powerful despite my current position.

His finger finally pushed inside me, and I gasped at the intrusion, my inner walls immediately clenching around the digit like they were trying to pull him deeper.

"More," I breathed against his mouth. "Please, I need—"

"I know what you need," Samson interrupted, adding a second finger and curling them inside me in a way that made stars explode behind my eyes. "But we're doing this my way, remember?"

I wrapped my legs tighter around him, using my position on the counter as leverage to pull him closer, to rub myself against his trapped erection. If I could just get close enough, if I could just maneuver the right way, I could position his cock against my entrance and—

But Samson was too experienced, too controlled to be manipulated so easily. He pulled his fingers out of me with a wet sound that made my face flush, and before I could protest, he was kneeling on the tiled floor in front of me.

I looked down at him in confusion for only a split second before realization dawned.

"Samson—" I started, but whatever I'd been about to say dissolved into a moan as he pushed my dress up around my waist and his head disappeared beneath the fabric.

I braced my hands on the counter behind me and leaned back, my head tilting toward the ceiling as I felt him hook his fingers into my panties and pull them aside. The cool air of the bathroom hit my exposed pussy for just a moment before his mouth was on me, and rational thought became impossible.

His tongue was everywhere at once—lapping at the arousal coating my inner thighs, dragging through my folds, circling my clit with agonizing precision. He ate me like a man starving, like I was the most delicious thing he'd ever tasted, and the wet sounds of his mouth on my pussy filled the bathroom, making me wetter.

I placed my feet on his shoulders for balance and let myself sink backward until my back touched the cool mirror behind me, spreading myself even more open for him. The position left me completely vulnerable, completely at his mercy, and I loved it.

A sudden sound—someone trying the bathroom door handle—made my heart leap into my throat.

The handle rattled again, and a woman's voice called out, "Is someone in there?"

I bit down hard on my lip to keep from crying out, my entire body tensing. But Samson didn't stop. If anything, the interruption seemed to spur him on. His tongue worked faster, pressing harder against my clit, and I had to cover my mouth with both hands to muffle the whimpers threatening to escape.

"I'll just wait," the voice said, sounding slightly annoyed.

Oh God. There was someone standing right outside the door while Samson Lang had his face buried between my legs.

The wrongness of it, the risk, the sheer audacity—it all combined to send a fresh surge of arousal through me. My hips moved of their own accord, grinding against Samson's mouth while I desperately tried to stay quiet.

He gripped my clit gently between his teeth and flicked his tongue over it rapidly, and I had to bite down on my palm to keep from screaming. The sensation was overwhelming, pleasure so intense it bordered on pain, and I could feel my orgasm building with terrifying speed.

My free hand found its way to my breasts, and I massaged them through the fabric of my dress, wishing I could get to my nipples but settling for the pressure and friction through the material. They were already hard, straining against my bra, adding another layer of sensation to the overwhelming experience.

"Oh my God," I whispered harshly, barely audible even to my own ears. My thighs were trembling now, my whole body coiling tighter and tighter like a spring about to release.

Samson hummed his approval, and the vibration against my sensitive flesh was my undoing.

"Fuck me," I begged in a desperate whisper. "Please, Samson, I need you to—"

But he ignored my plea, his tongue relentless as it drove me higher and higher toward the edge. My inner walls began throbbing, clenching around nothing, desperately empty and aching to be filled.

The orgasm hit me like a freight train.

I covered my mouth with both hands and screamed into my palms as pleasure exploded through every nerve ending in my body. My pussy flooded with release, and I used my legs to pull Samson's face harder against me, riding out the waves as they crashed over me again and again.

"Oh my God, yes, yes, yes," I chanted under my breath, my voice muffled by my hands but still too loud, too revealing.

The pleasure seemed to go on forever, each pulse sending aftershocks through my trembling body. Samson didn't let up until I was boneless and gasping, my legs falling open limply, unable to maintain the pressure anymore.

As the euphoria finally began to fade, I felt weak and disoriented, floating somewhere outside my body. Through the haze, I felt Samson slide my panties back into place—the lace now soaked and uncomfortable against my oversensitized flesh—and extract himself from beneath my dress.

He stood, looking completely composed despite what had just happened, and calmly zipped his pants back up. I stared at him in a daze, my mind struggling to process the fact that once again, he hadn't actually fucked me. He'd brought me to orgasm with his mouth, left himself hard and wanting, and seemed perfectly content with that arrangement.

Why? What was his endgame?

Samson smirked at me and wiped his mouth with his fingers, then licked them clean with a deliberateness that sent another flutter of arousal through my exhausted body.

"Delicious," he murmured, his eyes dancing with satisfaction and something that might have been affection.

He held his hand out to me, and I accepted it with movements that felt lazy and uncoordinated. My limbs didn't quite want to obey commands yet. Samson helped me down from the counter, steadying me when my legs wobbled, and I had to lean against him for a moment while the world stopped spinning.

"Straighten your dress," he instructed softly, and I looked down to realize the fabric was bunched around my waist, leaving me essentially exposed from the waist down.

I smoothed it back into place with shaking hands, hyperaware of the dampness of my panties and the way my legs still trembled with aftershocks.

"I'll meet you back at the table," Samson said, already moving toward the door. "Give it a few minutes. We don't want to be too obvious."

He cracked the door open and peered out, checking to make sure the coast was clear. Apparently satisfied, he slipped out of the bathroom without another word, leaving me alone with my racing heart and spinning thoughts.

I turned to the mirror and saw the evidence of what we'd done written all over my face.

My lipstick was smudged, the carefully applied red now faded and uneven. My eyes were bright, pupils dilated, my cheeks flushed with a post-orgasmic glow that couldn't be mistaken for anything else. My hair was slightly messed, a few strands falling out of Josie's careful styling.

I looked thoroughly ravished.

I grabbed my clutch and pulled out the lipstick Josie had lent me, carefully reapplying it and fixing the smudges. I smoothed down my hair, tucked the errant strands back into place, and took several deep breaths to try to calm my racing pulse.

By the time I was done, I looked almost presentable again. Almost like a woman who'd simply used the restroom, not one who'd just had the orgasm of her life on a marble countertop while a man ate her out.

I unlocked the door and stepped out into the hallway—

And nearly collided with an elderly woman who'd clearly been waiting.

"Finally," she huffed, giving me a look that was equal parts annoyance and knowing disapproval. "Some people have no consideration."

Heat flooded my face. "I'm so sorry, I—"

But she was already pushing past me into the bathroom, muttering something under her breath about "young people these days."

I fled back to the dining area, my heart pounding with a mixture of embarrassment and exhilaration.

CHAPTER 14

Samson was already seated at our table, looking completely unruffled, as if nothing unusual had happened. He was checking his phone with the casual air of someone who'd simply stepped away for a business call.

When I slid into my seat across from him, he looked up and smiled—a small, private smile that was just for me.

"Everything all right?" he asked innocuously, though his eyes gleamed with mischief.

"Perfect," I managed, my voice only slightly breathless.

Mindy appeared moments later with a to-go box containing what I assumed was our tiramisu, along with the check. Samson handed her a credit card without even looking at the total, and she departed with promises of a speedy return.

"Did you enjoy your dinner?" Samson asked, still with that innocent tone that completely contradicted the heat in his gaze.

"Very much." I met his eyes directly, refusing to be embarrassed. "All of it."

His smile widened. "Good. I'm glad."

Mindy returned with his card and the receipt, which he signed with a flourish before standing and offering me his hand. I took it and let him guide me out of the restaurant, acutely aware of the eyes that followed our progress.

Did they know? Could they tell what we'd done in their bathroom? The thought mortified me.

"Madison?"

I froze mid-step, my entire body going rigid. I didn't need to turn around to know who it was. That voice had been part of my life for two years, and even now, days after our explosive breakup, I recognized it immediately.

Jason.

Every instinct screamed at me to keep walking, to pretend I hadn't heard, to escape before this evening could be ruined. But something—pride, maybe, or just morbid curiosity—made me turn around.

Samson turned with me, his arm still wrapped around mine in a way that suddenly felt less like gentlemanly courtesy and more like possessive claim.

Jason was storming toward us, and as he got closer, I noticed he was wearing a uniform—black slacks and a button-down shirt with Rossini's elegant logo embroidered on the breast pocket. My stomach sank.

Of course. Of course he worked here now. Because the universe had a truly sadistic sense of humor, and on a night that had been going so perfectly, it had decided to throw my cheating ex-boyfriend directly into my path.

"What the hell is this?" Jason demanded, his voice loud enough to draw attention from nearby tables. His face was flushed, his eyes bouncing between me and Samson with an expression that mixed shock, anger, and something that looked almost like betrayal— which was rich, coming from him.

"Mind your own business, Jason," I snapped, trying to keep my voice level despite the way my heart was racing.

"You're out with someone already?" He was getting louder now, drawing even more stares. "It's been less than a week, Madison! And who the fuck is this guy? Your new fuck buddy? Is this why—"

His words cut off abruptly as Samson turned his full attention to Jason, and I watched my ex-boyfriend's face transform from anger to something approaching terror.

Recognition had dawned.

"Mr. W-Wolf," Jason stuttered, taking an involuntary step backward. "I didn't—I mean, I didn't know—"

"It's Lang, actually," Samson corrected coolly, his voice carrying the kind of quiet authority that made grown men reconsider their life choices. "Mr. Lang. And I have to ask—is this how you speak to all women, or just the ones who are far too good for you?"

Jason's mouth opened and closed soundlessly, his earlier bravado completely evaporated. Up close, I could see he looked terrible—bloodshot eyes, unkempt hair, the beginnings of a beard that suggested he'd stopped caring about grooming. He looked like he'd been drinking, though hopefully not while on duty.

"He's quite talkative when he's insulting women," Samson observed, glancing at me with amusement dancing in his eyes. "Not too bright, though, is he?"

"Hey!" Jason's indignation flared back up, fueled by wounded pride and possibly liquid courage. "I'm not an idiot."

"Clearly," Samson said with such dry, condescending sarcasm that I had to bite my lip to keep from laughing.

"Just because you have money doesn't make you better than me," Jason spat, his hands clenching into fists at his sides. For a terrifying moment, I thought he might actually try to hit Samson, and I tensed, ready to intervene.

"No, you're absolutely right," Samson agreed mildly. "My money doesn't make me better than you. What makes me better than you is that I am a man—a man who understands respect and integrity—while you are nothing more than a boy who shaves. Now," his voice dropped into a tone that brooked no argument. "Apologize to Madison for your crude language and your presumptuous behavior."

Jason scoffed, his face twisting into an ugly sneer I'd never seen before our breakup. "No." He crossed his arms over his chest in a gesture of defiance that looked childish rather than strong.

Samson was silent for a moment, and I could practically feel him recalibrating, deciding how to handle this situation. Then he turned to me with a smile that didn't reach his eyes.

"Shall we go, darling? We should leave the janitor to get back to his important work."

The casual dismissal was more cutting than any insult could have been. I giggled—I couldn't help it—and nodded, which clearly enraged Jason even more.

"I'm not a fucking janitor," he snarled, his voice rising to a near-shout. Several diners were openly staring now, and I saw the maître d' starting to move in our direction, clearly concerned about the disturbance.

Jason reached out and grabbed Samson's shoulder, spinning him around.

Everything happened very fast after that.

Samson whirled with a speed that seemed impossible for someone in a tailored suit, catching Jason's wrist and twisting it, forcing Jason to cry out. In one smooth motion, Samson released the wrist and gripped the front of Jason's shirt instead, using his momentum and Jason's off-balance stance to force him backward against the nearest table.

Jason fell onto the table's surface with a crash that sent empty plates and wine glasses scattering. One glass shattered on the floor, the sound sharp and final in the suddenly silent restaurant.

Samson leaned down, his face inches from Jason's, and when he spoke, his voice was low and deadly calm—far more terrifying than any shout could have been.

"If you ever lay a hand on me again," Samson said, each word precisely enunciated, "I will ruin your entire life. I will have you fired from this job and every other job in this town. I will make sure that your name becomes synonymous with unemployable. I will ensure that you spend the rest of your pathetic existence regretting the moment you thought you could touch me. Do we have an understanding?"

Jason's earlier bluster had completely vanished. His face had gone pale, his eyes wide with genuine fear. He swallowed hard and nodded frantically, looking like he might actually cry.

"I asked you a question," Samson pressed. "Do we have an understanding?"

"Yes," Jason gasped. "Yes, sir. I'm sorry. I'm so sorry."

Samson released him and stepped back, smoothing down the front of his jacket where Jason had wrinkled it. His face was completely calm again, as if the brief display of force had never happened.

"Madison," he said, turning to me and offering his arm once more. "Shall we?"

I took his arm, still slightly stunned by how quickly Samson had neutralized the situation. As we walked toward the exit, I couldn't resist glancing back.

Jason was still on the table, surrounded by broken glass and the concerned attention of the maître d' and several other staff members. He looked small and pathetic, and I felt a surge of satisfaction that I probably shouldn't have felt but couldn't bring myself to regret.

The cool night air hit us as we stepped outside, a sharp contrast to the warmth of the restaurant. I shivered involuntarily, and Samson immediately pulled me closer, wrapping an arm around my shoulders. His body heat was a welcome sensation, chasing away the chill.

"Are you all right?" he asked quietly.

"I'm fine. Better than fine, actually." I looked up at him, seeing his face illuminated by the soft lighting from the restaurant's entrance. "Thank you for that. For defending me."

"He was disrespectful," Samson said simply. "I don't tolerate disrespect, particularly not toward someone under my protection."

Under my protection. The phrase sent a warm flutter through my chest.

His driver appeared and opened my door. I slid into the car's luxurious interior, immediately surrounded by the scent of leather and expensive cologne. Samson followed a moment later, settling into the seat beside me and placing his hand on my knee.

The touch was casual, almost absent-minded, but it sent heat pooling in my belly.

"I'm guessing that was your boyfriend?" Samson asked as the car pulled out of the parking lot.

"Ex-boyfriend," I corrected firmly.

"Mm. A real winner, that one." There was amusement in his voice, and something else—satisfaction, maybe, at having put Jason in his place.

"Yeah, well..." I trailed off, not sure how to explain what I'd ever seen in Jason that had made me waste two years of my life on him.

"Did you mean what you said in there?" I asked suddenly.

"Which part are you referring to? I said several things."

"About how he treats women. How you said I was too good for him."

Samson was quiet for a moment, his thumb tracing absent circles on my knee. "Of course I meant it. You're way above him in every way that matters. Intelligence, grace, integrity—you have all the qualities he lacks. And you're far too beautiful for someone as ugly as he is, both inside and out."

I didn't think Jason was physically ugly—objectively, he was decent-looking—but there was an ugliness to his behavior, to the way he'd cheated and lied and then tried to make it my fault. An ugliness that Samson had seen immediately and called out without hesitation.

"Thank you," I said softly.

The car was heading somewhere, though I wasn't paying attention to the route. I assumed Samson was taking me home, that our evening was over, that I'd be returned to my cold, empty apartment to process everything that had happened.

But I wasn't ready for it to be over. Not yet.

And more importantly, I wasn't ready to leave Samson without returning the pleasure he'd given me twice now—first in his office, then in the restaurant bathroom—while denying himself both times.

I leaned over into his lap without giving myself time to second-guess the impulse, my hands moving to the front of his pants. Samson made a small sound of surprise that quickly transformed into a groan of approval as I rubbed my palms against his thighs, working my way up toward the bulge I could already feel hardening beneath the expensive fabric.

"Madison," he said, his voice rough. "What are you—"

"Returning a favor," I interrupted, looking up at him through my lashes while my fingers found his zipper. "You've made me come twice. It seems only fair that I return the gesture."

His hand slid down my back until it reached my ass, where he squeezed hard enough to make me gasp, then delivered a sharp slap that sent sparks of sensation through me.

"Fair has nothing to do with it," he said. "But I'm not going to stop you."

I freed his cock from his pants, and even in the dim light of the car's interior, I could see how hard he was, how much he'd wanted this all evening. The sight sent a surge of power through me—I'd done this to him, my body and my presence had affected him this much.

I stroked him slowly, learning the shape and weight of him in my hand. He was long and thick, definitely bigger than Jason had been, and the comparison made me smile. Of course Samson Lang would be impressive in every way, including this.

I leaned down and started licking his crown, swirling my tongue around the sensitive ridge. Samson's hand wove into my hair, not forcing but guiding, and I heard his breathing change, becoming heavier and less controlled.

I licked my lips to wet them, then wrapped my mouth around his cock and took him as deep as I could manage on the first try. The taste of him flooded my senses.

"Fuck," Samson breathed, his hips shifting beneath me. "Your mouth feels incredible."

The praise spurred me on. I started bobbing my head up and down his length, gradually taking him deeper with each descent, trying to relax my throat and suppress my gag reflex. The wet sounds of my mouth on his cock filled the car, obscene and arousing in equal measure.

There was no real reason to hurry—the driver couldn't see us through the privacy partition, and I had no idea how long the drive would be—but I found myself desperate to make Samson lose control. To see him come undone the way he'd made me come undone.

I wanted to taste him, to feel his release on my tongue, to swallow him down and know that I'd given him the same intense pleasure he'd given me.

I lifted my head off his cock and let saliva drip from my mouth onto his shaft, using it as lubricant as I wrapped my hand around his thickness and stroked him firmly. Samson groaned in response, his fingers tightening in my hair.

I focused my attention on the spot just below his crown, knowing from experience that this was often the most sensitive area. My grip was tight, my strokes quick and efficient, and I watched with satisfaction as Samson's hips started jerking involuntarily, his careful control slipping.

A bead of precum appeared at his tip, glistening in the low light, and I leaned down to lick it off. The taste was different from Jason's—cleaner, somehow, less bitter. Or maybe that was just my mind attributing positive qualities to everything about Samson.

I wrapped my other hand around the base of his shaft, creating a seal, and worked both hands in rhythm while keeping my mouth close to his tip, ready to take him in again.

Samson's movements were becoming more frantic now, less controlled. His breathing was ragged, his hand in my hair alternating between pulling me closer and pushing me away as if he couldn't decide whether he wanted more or needed me to stop.

"Madison," he warned, his voice strained. "If you don't want—fuck—if you don't want me to come in your mouth, you need to—"

But that was exactly what I wanted.

I released the hand at his base and wrapped my mouth around his cock, taking him deep, and felt his shaft pulse and thicken. For a brief, wicked moment, I tightened my remaining grip, holding back his release, making him suffer just a little longer.

"Oh fuck," Samson hissed through clenched teeth, his entire body going rigid.

Then I released my grip and took him as deep as I could manage.

Thick, hot ropes of cum flooded my mouth, coating my tongue with a taste that was salty and slightly sweet and entirely addictive. I swallowed quickly and kept bobbing my head, milking him for every drop, determined not to waste any of it.

Samson's hand tightened almost painfully in my hair, holding me in place while he emptied himself into my mouth with soft groans that sent shivers of satisfaction through me.

When I was certain he'd finished, when his cock had stopped pulsing and his grip on my hair had relaxed, I slowly pulled off him and sat back up in my seat. I licked my lips, savoring the last traces of his taste, and met his eyes with a small, satisfied smile.

Samson looked thoroughly debauched. His hair was messed from where I'd run my hands through it, his face flushed, his breathing still coming in slightly ragged gasps. He looked at me with an expression I'd never seen before—something between awe and hunger and something that might have been tenderness.

"That was..." he started, then seemed to lose the words.

"Fair?" I suggested, echoing his earlier comment.

He laughed, a genuine sound that transformed his entire face. "Devastating. You're going to be the death of me, Madison Carter."

I settled back into my seat properly, acutely aware of the dampness of my own panties and the ache between my legs that his orgasm had done nothing to satisfy. I'd gotten him off, yes, but it had only made me want him more.

One more day, I reminded myself. One more day in our contract, and surely, surely, he would finally fuck me properly. Would fill me the way I'd been craving since this all started. Would come inside my pussy instead of on my back or in my mouth.

The thought made me clench involuntarily, and I shifted in my seat, trying to alleviate the pressure.

"Uncomfortable?" Samson asked, noticing my fidgeting. His hand returned to my thigh, higher this time, his fingers playing with the hem of my dress.

"A little," I admitted.

"We could do something about that," he suggested, his fingers inching higher. "I could return the favor right here in the car."

For a moment, I was tempted. God, I was tempted. But some part of me wanted to wait, wanted to save that desperate need for the last day of our contract. Wanted our final encounter to be fueled by days of built-up desire and anticipation.

"Save it," I said, catching his hand before it could reach its destination. "For next time."

His eyes darkened with promise. "Next time," he agreed.

CHAPTER 15

The car was slowing now, and I looked out the window to see familiar surroundings. We were approaching my neighborhood, my street, my sad little house with its broken heat and water heater.

The contrast between the luxury I'd been experiencing all evening and the reality I was about to return to was almost physically painful.

We pulled into my driveway, and the driver exited and came around to open my door, but before I could step out, Samson caught my hand and pulled me back for a kiss.

It wasn't like the desperate, hungry kisses we'd shared in the restaurant bathroom. This was slower, deeper, more deliberate. His hand cupped my jaw, his thumb stroking my cheek, and I melted into him with a soft sound that was somewhere between a sigh and a moan.

When we finally broke apart, we were both breathing hard, and the desire to drag him inside with me was almost overwhelming.

"Do you want to come in?" I asked before I could think better of it.

It was a stupid question. My house was freezing, with no heat and no hot water. It was small and shabby and probably looked like a hovel compared to wherever Samson lived. But I wanted him here anyway, wanted to wake up in his arms, wanted to spend the night exploring every inch of each other without time limits or contracts hanging over us.

Samson's expression softened, and for a moment, I thought he might actually say yes. But then he shook his head with what looked like genuine regret.

"I would love to," he said quietly. "But I can't. I have paperwork that needs to be finished for a meeting tomorrow morning. If I don't review it tonight, the deal could fall through."

Disappointment flooded through me, sharp and unexpected in its intensity. Part of me had been hoping—fantasizing, really—that he would say yes. That we'd spend the night tangled in my sheets, fucking until neither of us had the energy to move, forgetting about contracts and arrangements and all the complicated reasons this was supposed to be purely transactional.

But another part of me was relieved. If Samson came inside, he'd see how I really lived. The broken heat, the cold water, the way I had to layer blankets to stay warm at night. He'd see the water stains on the ceiling from the leak I couldn't afford to fix, the ancient appliances that barely worked, all the evidence of my poverty laid bare.

And given how kind he'd been tonight— defending me against Jason, taking me to an expensive restaurant, treating me like I actually mattered—there was no telling how he might react. He'd probably offer to fix everything, to throw money at my problems until they disappeared.

And I didn't want his charity. Didn't want to be another debt he held over me, another obligation I owed him.

I just wanted... him. Just him, without all the complications.

"All right," I said, trying to keep the disappointment out of my voice. "I understand."

"I'll call you," Samson promised. "For the third day. Soon."

"See you tomorrow?" I asked hopefully, even though I knew it was unlikely.

Samson only smiled at me, that enigmatic expression that could mean anything or nothing, and I had to accept that as the only answer I was going to get.

I stepped out of the car, and the driver—whose name I still didn't know—walked me to my door with the same professional courtesy he'd shown all evening. He waited until I had my key in the lock, gave me a small nod, then returned to the car.

I watched from my doorway as the car backed out of my driveway and disappeared down the dark street, its taillights fading into the distance. Part of me wanted to run after it, to change my mind and beg Samson to stay or to take me home with him instead.

But I didn't. I just stood there, dressed in borrowed finery, watching until the car was completely out of sight.

Only then did I step inside and close the door behind me.

The house was dark, and I fumbled for the light switch, my fingers clumsy from the cold and the lingering effects of too much wine and not enough food. The light flickered on, illuminating my small, cramped living room with its secondhand furniture and—

Wait.

The lights were already on in the kitchen. I could see the glow spilling out from the doorway, casting shadows across the worn carpet.

Fear gripped me, sudden and visceral.

Someone was in my house.

My first thought was Jason. Had he somehow gotten in? Did he still have a key from when we were dating? My mind flashed to his rage-twisted face at the restaurant, the way he'd grabbed Marcus's shoulder, the violence barely restrained beneath his surface.

What if he'd come here to wait for me? To confront me again, drunk and angry and looking for someone to blame for his shitty life?

I pulled my phone from the clutch Josie had lent me, my hands shaking as I tried to unlock it and call 911.

The screen stayed dark. Dead battery.

"Damn it," I whispered, my heart pounding so hard I could feel it in my throat.

I should leave. Should run back outside and pound on a neighbor's door, beg to use their phone, get help. But what if I was wrong? What if it was nothing, just a light I'd accidentally left on, and I was about to wake up the whole neighborhood over my own paranoia?

I crept toward the kitchen as quietly as I could in my heels, trying to remember if I owned anything I could use as a weapon. A knife from the kitchen, maybe? But that would mean getting past whoever was in there first.

I rounded the corner into the living room, my muscles coiled and ready to run—

And a small figure stepped out of the kitchen doorway.

I almost screamed, the sound catching in my throat and coming out as a strangled gasp. My heart felt like it was going to burst out of my chest. I staggered backward, my heel catching on the edge of the carpet—

"Madison?"

The familiar voice stopped me mid-panic, and my eyes finally focused on the figure in front of me.

Grandma.

"Are you all right, dear?" she asked, concern creasing her weathered face. "You look like you've seen a ghost."

"Grandma!" I pressed a hand to my chest, trying to slow my racing heart. "You almost gave me a heart attack! I thought you were a burglar or—or Jason or something!"

She chuckled, the sound warm and comforting in a way that made my eyes sting with unexpected tears. "Why on earth would you think that? It's Thursday night."

Thursday night.

The words hit me like a physical blow, and I felt my stomach drop as realization crashed over me in a wave of guilt and embarrassment.

Thursday. Our standing dinner night. The tradition we'd maintained for years, alternating between her house and mine, a weekly check-in that was as much about connection as it was about food.

And this week, it was my turn to host.

I'd completely, utterly forgotten.

I'd been so focused on Samson, so consumed by our arrangement and my confusing feelings and the anticipation of seeing him again, that I'd let our dinner completely slip my mind. Grandma had probably been sitting here waiting for me, wondering where I was, worrying that something had happened.

"Oh my God," I groaned, putting my hand to my forehead. "I'm so sorry. I completely forgot. I've been so—there's been so much going on, and I just—I'm so sorry."

"I tried calling you," Grandma said gently, with no reproach in her voice even though I deserved it. "But it just went straight to voicemail."

Dead battery. Of course.

"I hope you don't mind that I let myself in with the spare key you gave me," she continued. "And I'm afraid I couldn't wait any longer. I got too hungry, so I went ahead and ate dinner without you. It's cold now, but I put the leftovers in your fridge if you want them."

The fact that she was apologizing to me—apologizing for eating in my house when I was the one who'd stood her up—made me feel even worse.

"You're fine," I said quickly. "This is entirely my fault. I'm so sorry, Grandma. Work has been... it's been crazy, and I lost track of what day it was."

"Work keeping you that busy?" she asked, studying my face in that way she had that always made me feel like she could see right through any lie.

"Something like that," I said vaguely.

She wrapped me in a hug, and I breathed in her familiar scent—lavender soap and the faint aroma of the cookies she was always baking. For a moment, I felt like a child again, safe and protected and loved unconditionally.

"I really am sorry," I murmured into her shoulder.

"Hush. It's all right, dear. Life gets busy sometimes." She pulled back and looked me up and down, taking in the dress, the heels, the makeup that was probably smudged by now. "Besides, you're all dressed up. Did you go out on a date tonight?"

There was a hopeful note in her voice, and I could see a small smile tugging at the corners of her mouth. She'd been worried about me since the breakup with Jason, I knew. Worried that I'd be alone, that I'd throw myself into work and never let myself be happy again.

If only she knew the truth.

"It's... complicated," I said finally, because I couldn't quite bring myself to say yes or no.

It technically wasn't a date. Samson and I had a contract, a business arrangement where I provided services in exchange for debt forgiveness. There was nothing romantic about it, at least not on paper.

But at the same time, there were feelings brewing inside me that I couldn't control or explain. Feelings that went way beyond physical attraction or gratitude for him saving Grandma's house. Real feelings, the kind that made my chest ache when I thought about our arrangement ending, about never seeing him again once the third day was complete.

If I said yes to Grandma's question, she'd want details. She'd want to know who I'd gone out with, where we'd gone, what my intentions were. And I couldn't tell her any of that without revealing the whole sordid truth about our arrangement.

If I said no, I'd be lying. And somehow, that felt worse.

"Ah," Grandma said, her eyes twinkling with understanding. "I know exactly what you mean. I had a few experiences like that when I was younger."

She settled onto the couch and patted the cushion beside her, clearly prepared to stay and talk. I kicked off the heels—my feet were killing me—and sat down, curling my legs beneath me.

"There was this man," Grandma began, launching into a story I'd heard variations of many times before. "His name was Thomas, and I met him when I was about your age. Twenty-three, I think. Or maybe twenty-four? The years all blur together now."

I'd heard about Thomas before—the man who wasn't Grandpa, the road not taken. But I'd never really paid attention to the story, had always been too young or too distracted to care about my grandmother's love life from fifty years ago.

Tonight, though, I listened intently, hoping that somewhere in her story I'd find clarity for my own situation.

"Thomas was so handsome," Grandma said, her eyes going distant with memory. "Tall, with dark hair and these eyes that seemed to see right through you. He was charming, always knew exactly what to say to make me laugh. And he was ambitious—he had big plans, big dreams. He wanted to travel the world, experience everything life had to offer."

She paused, a wistful smile on her face.

"He wanted me to come with him. To leave everything I knew and just... go. See the world together."

"Why didn't you?" I asked, genuinely curious now.

"I was scared," Grandma admitted. "Terrified, actually. I'd been born and raised here in this town. I'd never even left the state, let alone the country. And Thomas... he was talking about Paris and Tokyo and places I couldn't even pronounce. It seemed impossibly big, impossibly risky."

"So you chose Grandpa instead?"

"I did. Your grandfather was safe, you see. Predictable. He had a steady job at the mill, a house in town, roots that went deep. He wanted the same things I thought I wanted— a quiet life, kids, growing old in the same place we'd been young."

"Do you regret it?" I asked quietly.

Grandma was silent for a long moment, considering. "No," she said finally. "I loved your grandfather very much. We had a good life together, a good marriage. But sometimes..." She trailed off, her gaze distant. "Sometimes I wonder what might have happened if I'd been brave enough to say yes to Thomas. If I'd chosen passion over security."

The parallels to my own situation were impossible to ignore. Samson was exciting, dangerous, overwhelming—everything Jason had never been. But he was also my mother's ex-husband, a man twenty years older than me, someone whose world was so far removed from mine we might as well be different species.

And I was terrified. Of what people would think if they found out. Of losing control of my life to someone as dominant and powerful as Samson. Of falling for him only to discover it was all just physical for him, that I meant nothing beyond our contract.

"What were you so afraid of?" I asked. "With Thomas, I mean."

"Oh, so many things," Grandma said with a self-deprecating laugh. "I was afraid of leaving my family, of being so far from home. I was afraid that Thomas would get tired of me, that I wouldn't be interesting enough to hold his attention once the novelty wore off. I was afraid of not being in control, of putting my fate in someone else's hands."

She looked at me then, really looked at me, and I had the uncomfortable feeling she knew exactly why I was asking these questions.

"But mostly," she said softly, "I was afraid of how much I felt for him. It was so intense, so consuming. I'd never felt anything like that before, and it scared me. With your grandfather, my feelings grew slowly, comfortably. But with Thomas... it was like standing on the edge of a cliff, knowing one more step and I'd be falling."

"And you stepped back from the edge," I said.

"I did." She patted my hand. "And like I said, I don't regret it. I had a beautiful life with your grandfather. But Madison, dear— don't let fear be the only thing that makes your decisions for you. Sometimes the cliff is worth jumping off."

We stayed up late into the night talking, the conversation eventually drifting away from Thomas and into easier topics—town gossip, a new recipe she wanted to try, the book club she'd recently joined.

Around eleven, she shivered and pulled her cardigan tighter around herself.

"I must be getting old," she said with a rueful smile. "I'm freezing. Are you cold, dear?"

I was, actually. The house was like an icebox, and even with the layers of my dress, I was starting to get goosebumps. But I couldn't tell her that the heat was broken, that I'd been living like this for days now.

If Grandma knew, she'd insist I stay at her house. Would probably lecture me about taking care of myself, about not sacrificing my health to save money. And while the idea of a warm bed was incredibly tempting, I didn't have the energy to pack a bag and drive across town.

Besides, this was my home. Broken and cold and shabby as it was, it was mine, and I didn't want to abandon it.

"I'm okay," I lied. "But it is getting late. You should probably head home before it gets any later."

"You're right, you're right." She stood and gathered her things—her purse, the knitting project she'd brought with her. "I left the dinner in your fridge. Make sure you eat it tomorrow, all right? You're getting too thin."

"I will. I promise."

I walked her to the door and hugged her tightly, breathing in her comforting scent one more time.

"Thank you for understanding," I said. "About tonight. About me forgetting."

"Oh, sweetheart. Everyone forgets things sometimes. Just..." She pulled back and looked at me seriously. "Whatever this complicated situation is that you're in? Be careful. And remember that you can always come to me if you need to talk. About anything."

"I know. Thank you."

I watched from the doorway as she got into her car and backed carefully out of the driveway. She waved once before driving off, and I waved back, standing there until her taillights disappeared around the corner.

Then I closed the door, locked it, and leaned against it with a long, shaky exhale.

Alone again. Just me and my thoughts and the cold, empty house.

I wandered into the kitchen and opened the fridge to see what Grandma had made. A casserole of some kind, still in its baking dish, covered carefully with foil. My stomach growled despite the huge meal I'd had at Rossini's. Apparently giving Samson a blowjob had worked up an appetite.

I smiled at the memory, then caught sight of my reflection in the darkened kitchen window.

I still looked like the woman from earlier—hair styled, makeup intact, wearing a dress that probably cost more than my monthly rent. But underneath, I was still just Madison Carter. Still broke, still struggling, still desperately trying to hold my life together with duct tape and determination.

What would Samson think if he could see me now? Would he still look at me with that heat in his eyes? Or would he see what I really was—a girl playing dress-up in borrowed clothes, pretending to be something she wasn't?

I turned away from my reflection and headed to my bedroom, suddenly exhausted down to my bones.

I carefully removed the dress and hung it up, knowing I'd need to return it to Josie soon. The makeup came off next, leaving my face bare and plain. The elaborate hairstyle was dismantled, bobby pins scattered across my dresser as I brushed out the waves.

By the time I crawled into bed—still dressed in my nice underwear because I was too tired to change—I looked like myself again. Just Madison, no artifice, no pretense.

But as I lay there in the dark, wrapped in every blanket I owned, my mind wandered back to Samson. To his hands on my body, his mouth on mine, the way he'd looked at me over dinner like I was the most fascinating thing in the world.

Grandma's story kept playing through my mind, particularly that last part about fear being the thing that made her decision.

I was afraid. There was no point denying it anymore.

I was afraid of how much I wanted Samson, of how easily he'd slipped past my defenses and made me feel things I'd never felt before. I was afraid of the power imbalance between us, of the fact that he could destroy my life with a single phone call if he wanted to. I was afraid of what would happen when our arrangement ended, whether he'd just walk away without a backward glance while I was left picking up the pieces of my heart.

But underneath the fear was something else. Something that felt suspiciously like hope.

Hope that maybe, just maybe, Samson felt something for me too. That the way he'd defended me against Jason, the gentleness he'd shown at dinner, the way he'd held me after making me come—maybe all of that meant something beyond our contract.

The third day would tell me everything I needed to know.

Either Samson would fuck me and walk away, the debt paid and the arrangement complete, proving that this had always been just business for him.

Or... or something else might happen. Something I didn't dare hope for but couldn't stop myself from wanting.

I fell asleep still wondering, still afraid, still desperately hoping that when I jumped off the cliff, Samson would be there to catch me.

Or at least fall with me.

CHAPTER 16

The next day, I had to work the mid-day shift, which meant dragging myself out of bed after only a few hours of sleep.

I'd stayed awake far too late replaying every moment of the evening with Samson—the restaurant, the bathroom, the car ride home. My body had ached with unfulfilled desire, my mind spinning with questions about what it all meant, until exhaustion had finally pulled me under somewhere around three in the morning.

My alarm went off at nine, and I seriously considered calling in sick. But I needed the money, needed the distraction, and—if I was being honest—needed something to occupy my mind besides obsessive analysis of every word Samson had said and every look he'd given me.

So I hauled myself out of bed, took the world's fastest cold shower, and threw on my work uniform with movements that felt robotic and disconnected.

At least my car started without any drama. Small miracles.

I arrived at the hotel fifteen minutes early, the parking lot mostly empty at this hour. The mid-day shift was usually the quietest—checkout rush was over, most guests either out exploring or settled in their rooms. It meant fewer interruptions while I cleaned, which was normally a blessing.

Today, though, I could have used the distraction.

Josie was working the front desk, and when she saw me walk in, she immediately abandoned her post and followed me to the storage room where I was gathering supplies for my cleaning cart.

Which was weird, because Josie loved being at the front desk. She thrived on the interaction with guests, the small dramas of hotel life. The fact that she was following me instead suggested she had something on her mind.

Something she wanted to talk about.

But oddly, she wasn't talking. She just trailed behind me in uncharacteristic silence, watching as I loaded towels and cleaning products onto my cart with mechanical efficiency.

"You all right?" I asked finally, because the silence was starting to unnerve me. Josie quiet was like a tornado calm—usually a sign that something big was about to hit.

"Yeah, why?" she said, but her tone was off. Too casual, too forced.

"You're quiet today. That's not like you."

Josie pursed her lips, her eyes darting around like she was checking for eavesdroppers even though we were completely alone. I watched her internal struggle play out on her face—the desire to keep quiet warring with her natural tendency to gossip—and I knew with sinking certainty that whatever she was holding back was going to be bad.

I raised an eyebrow and waited, because I'd learned over the years that Josie couldn't keep secrets to save her life. If you just gave her enough silent space, she'd fill it.

I didn't have to wait long.

"Jason's telling everyone that you're fucking the Wolf!" she finally blurted out, the words exploding from her like they'd been physically painful to hold in.

My heart stopped. Literally stopped beating for a second before slamming back to life with a force that made my chest ache.

"He's what?" I managed, my voice coming out strangled.

"Yeah!" Josie was in full gossip mode now, the floodgates open. "He's been telling everyone—and I mean everyone—that he saw you with Samson Lang at Rossini's last night. He said you two were all over each other, that it was obvious you were sleeping together, that you've probably been cheating on him the whole time you were dating and that's why you freaked out when you caught him with Lindsey—"

"We were not all over each other," I interrupted, panic rising in my throat. "That's a complete exaggeration. We were just having dinner."

Josie gasped, her hand flying to her mouth in dramatic fashion. "Wait. So you *were* there with him? It's true?"

Shit. Shit, shit, shit.

I'd just confirmed the core of Jason's story without meaning to, and now Josie was looking at me with eyes as wide as saucers, practically vibrating with curiosity.

The fear I'd felt last night—the fear about losing control, about what people would think, about my private business becoming public entertainment—came flooding back with a vengeance. My hands trembled as I gripped the handle of the cleaning cart.

I should have known better. Should have anticipated this. Jason had always had a big mouth, had never understood the concept of discretion or privacy. Of course he'd gone running to tell everyone who'd listen about seeing me with Samson. It probably made him feel better about his own shitty behavior—if I was "cheating" with someone else, then his affair with Lindsey wasn't so bad, right?

"I was there with him, yes," I said slowly, carefully, trying to figure out how much I could reveal without exposing the whole arrangement. "But it's not what Jason's making it sound like."

"Then what is it?" Josie demanded. "Why were you having dinner with the Wolf? What happened? Are you two together? Are you sleeping with him?"

The questions came rapid-fire, barely giving me time to process one before the next hit. I blinked at her, my mind racing through possible explanations that wouldn't be complete lies but also wouldn't reveal the truth.

"We went to dinner. That's it. We're not— we're not together. And no, we're not sleeping together." The last part was technically true. We hadn't actually had sex yet, just... everything else.

"But why?" Josie pressed. "Why would you go to dinner with him?"

"You know he was my stepdad, right?" I said, deflecting as I pushed my cart toward the first room on my list. Maybe if I started working, Josie would get the hint and leave me alone.

No such luck. She followed me inside the room, closing the door behind her like we were having a private meeting.

"He *was* your stepdad," Josie corrected. "Past tense. Your mom left him years ago, and they're divorced now, so..." She let that hang in the air, heavy with implication.

"So what?" I asked, yanking the blanket and sheets off the bed with more force than necessary.

"So you could be sleeping with him without it being weird," Josie said bluntly. "Legally, I mean. It's not like anyone would blame you. I mean, Jesus, Madison—the man has money, power, looks. I'm sure he's incredible in bed. All that dominance and control? That translates, trust me."

Heat flooded my face, because she wasn't wrong about that last part. Not that I could tell her that.

"I wouldn't know," I said, which was the truth if you parsed it very specifically. Samson hadn't actually fucked me yet, so I genuinely didn't know what he was like in bed. Just what he was like with his mouth and hands and words, which was already better than anything I'd experienced before.

Josie stared at me for a long moment, her eyes narrowed like she was trying to read my expression, trying to determine if I was lying or telling the truth.

"I want to know if something's going on," she said finally, her voice softening into something that sounded almost hurt. "We're friends, Madison. Friends tell each other everything. *Everything*."

"I know," I said quietly, feeling guilt twist in my stomach.

And I did want to tell her. God, I wanted to tell someone about this impossible situation I'd gotten myself into. About the contract and the arrangement and the way Samson made me feel things I'd never felt before. About how scared and excited and confused I was all at the same time.

But the contract had a confidentiality clause. I couldn't tell anyone that Samson was essentially paying me for my time, that this was a transaction with specific terms and conditions. If word got out, it wouldn't just ruin my reputation—it could potentially cause legal problems for Marcus, damage his business, create a scandal that would touch everyone involved.

Including Grandma, whose house this was all supposed to save.

The words were right on the tip of my tongue when I heard a car pull into the parking lot, the sound of tires on gravel audible through the open window.

Josie groaned. "Gotta go work," she complained, shooting me a look that clearly said this conversation wasn't over. Then she was gone, leaving me alone with my thoughts and my half-made bed.

I finished putting the fitted sheet on and tried to focus on the task at hand, but my mind kept wandering back to last night. To Samson on his knees in front of me in that bathroom, his head disappearing under my dress. To the way his tongue had felt against my clit, the way he'd hummed his approval while eating me out like I was the most delicious thing he'd ever tasted.

My pussy clenched at the memory, and I felt heat pooling low in my belly.

God, he'd been incredible. That orgasm had been one of the best of my life—intense and overwhelming and so good I'd barely been able to stay quiet with someone waiting right outside the door.

And we still hadn't actually had sex.

The anticipation was killing me. I wanted our last day together to happen now, wanted to finally feel his cock inside me, wanted to know what it would be like to have Samson Lang fuck me properly instead of just teasing me to the edge of madness.

I clenched my walls again and looked toward the door, an absolutely crazy thought forming in my mind.

I was alone. The room was locked. Josie was busy at the front desk. I had at least fifteen minutes before I needed to move on to the next room.

I could...

My hand moved to the door before I could second-guess the impulse, turning the deadbolt with a soft click. Then I was moving toward the bathroom, my heart pounding with a mixture of anticipation and disbelief at what I was about to do.

This wasn't like me. I didn't masturbate at work. I didn't take risks like this, didn't let desire override my practical nature.

But Samson had changed something in me. Had awakened something that couldn't be pushed back down no matter how hard I tried.

I closed the bathroom door even though I was alone in the locked room, some part of me needing that extra layer of privacy. Then I shimmied out of my work pants and draped them over the shower curtain rod, leaving me in just my underwear and work shirt.

My reflection in the mirror looked flushed, eyes bright with arousal, lips parted with quick breathing. I looked like someone about to do something reckless.

I looked like someone who didn't care.

I planted one foot on the edge of the bathtub for balance and let my hand drift between my legs, fingers brushing against the damp fabric of my underwear. I was already wet, had been wet since the moment Josie mentioned Samson's name, my body responding to just the thought of him.

I pushed my panties aside and found my clit, circling it with gentle pressure that made my breath hitch. My eyes fell closed, and immediately I was back in that restaurant bathroom with Samson's hands on my thighs, his mouth on my pussy, his voice telling me I was a good girl.

A wave of heat washed over me, and I increased the pressure, my fingers moving in tight circles that made my legs tremble. I'd never done anything like this before—never been so desperate for release that I couldn't wait until I got home, couldn't make it through a work shift without touching myself.

But this need for Samson was primal, consuming, impossible to ignore.

My free hand gripped the edge of the sink for balance as my legs started to shake. Images flashed through my mind—Samson's dark eyes watching me come undone, his fingers inside me, his cock in my mouth, the way he'd looked at me over dinner like I was the only person in the world who mattered.

"Fuck," I groaned, trying to keep my voice low even though I was alone. My walls clenched around nothing, desperately empty, aching to be filled.

I needed him. Needed to feel him inside me, needed to know what it would be like when he finally stopped teasing and actually fucked me the way I'd been craving.

My fingers moved faster, my hips rocking against my hand, chasing the pleasure that was building at the base of my spine. It was crazy how much he'd changed me in just a few days, how thoroughly he'd gotten under my skin and rewired my entire system.

My orgasm hit suddenly, pleasure crashing through me in waves that made my knees buckle. I had to brace myself against the sink with both hands to keep from falling, my pussy clenching and releasing as I came with Samson's name on my lips.

I stayed bent over the sink for a long moment, breathing hard, my body still trembling with aftershocks. As the pleasure faded and clarity returned, I was hit with the full realization of what I'd just done.

I'd masturbated in a hotel bathroom. At work. While guests were literally in rooms next door.

"Jesus Christ, Madison," I muttered to my reflection. "What is he doing to you?"

But I knew the answer. Samson was systematically dismantling every defense I had, every rule I'd set for myself, every line I'd sworn I wouldn't cross. And the terrifying part was that I was letting him. More than that—I was actively participating, throwing myself into this arrangement with an enthusiasm that should have embarrassed me but instead just made me want more.

I cleaned myself up, washed my hands thoroughly, and put my pants back on. By the time I emerged from the bathroom, I looked relatively normal again—just a hotel maid finishing up a room, nothing unusual to see here.

I unlocked the door and peeked out into the hallway. Empty. Thank God.

I finished the room in record time and moved on to the next one, then the next, working with mechanical efficiency while my mind spun through scenarios for tonight. Because Samson would call. He had to. We only had one day left in our contract, and he wasn't the type to let something like that slip through his fingers.

Tonight. It would be tonight. And when he finally fucked me—

My phone buzzed in my pocket, making me jump. I pulled it out and saw Josie's name on the screen.

You disappeared. Everything ok?

I texted back: *Fine. Just focused on work.*

Her response came immediately: *We're still talking about this later. I want details!!!*

I sighed and shoved my phone back in my pocket. Josie wasn't going to let this go, and I was going to have to come up with a better cover story than "we're just friends" because nobody was going to believe that, least of all someone as perceptive as Josie.

But I'd worry about that later. Right now, I needed to get through my shift without thinking about Samson every five seconds. An impossible task, it turned out.

The rest of the day passed in a blur of cleaning and avoiding Josie's pointed questions whenever our paths crossed. She tried to corner me twice more, but I managed to deflect both times by pointing out actual guests who needed help or rooms that urgently needed attention.

By the time my shift ended at five, I was exhausted and keyed up in equal measure, my body aching from physical labor and sexual frustration.

Josie was clocking out at the same time, and she followed me to the parking lot like a persistent shadow.

"What are you doing tonight?" she asked as we approached our cars.

"I don't know yet," I lied, because I had no idea what Samson had planned but I knew with absolute certainty I'd be doing whatever he asked. "Why?"

"Joseph's throwing a party at his parents' cabin. He said to invite anyone interested." She waggled her eyebrows suggestively. "You could bring your mystery dinner date."

I couldn't help but laugh at the mental image of Samson at one of Joseph's notorious parties—keg stands and beer pong and people making terrible decisions in sleeping bags. Samson, who probably drank wine that cost more than the entire party budget, surrounded by drunk twenty-somethings.

"Thanks, but I think I'll pass this time," I said.

"Your loss." Josie grinned. "Though it would cause quite a stir if you showed up with the Wolf. Can you imagine?"

She laughed and got into her car, leaving me standing in the parking lot shaking my head.

Bring Samson to a party. Right. As if.

I pulled out my phone as I walked to my car, intending to check the time, and noticed I had a missed call. From an unknown number.

No, not unknown. A number I recognized, even though I'd never saved it in my contacts.

Samson.

My heart rate spiked as I saw he'd left a voicemail. I fumbled with the phone, nearly dropping it in my haste to access my messages, and pressed it to my ear with trembling hands.

His voice filled my ear, smooth and confident: "Tonight. The Den. Nine o'clock sharp. Don't be late."

That was it. Short, direct, commanding. So perfectly Samson that I couldn't help but smile even as my stomach did a nervous flip.

I played it again. And again. And again, just enjoying the sound of his voice, the way he said "don't be late" like he knew I'd be counting down the minutes.

Tonight.

It was finally going to happen. Our third and final day. The culmination of everything that had been building between us.

Samson was going to fuck me.

The thought sent a shiver through my entire body—part anticipation, part nervousness, part desperate, aching need.

I had four hours to get ready. Four hours to make myself look perfect, to prepare myself mentally and physically for whatever Samson had planned.

Four hours until I found out if this arrangement meant anything beyond a contract, or if I was about to have my heart broken by a man who'd paid for the privilege of using my body.

I got in my car and started the engine, already mentally cataloging what I needed to do.

Shower. Hair. Makeup. Something to wear—something that would drive Samson crazy when he saw me.

Four hours.

I could do this.

I had to do this.

Because one way or another, tonight would change everything.

CHAPTER 17

I rushed home with a sense of urgency that bordered on manic, even though I had nearly four hours before I needed to be at the Den.

But I couldn't sit still. Couldn't calm down. Couldn't think about anything except Samson and what was about to happen tonight.

This was it. The final day of our contract. The culmination of everything that had been building between us. And I wanted it to be perfect—wanted to look perfect, feel perfect, be everything he wanted and more.

The cold shower was brutal as always, but I barely registered the icy spray. My mind was elsewhere, running through scenarios of how tonight might go. Would Samson take me on that expensive rug again? Bend me over his desk? Press me against the windows overlooking the city while he fucked me from behind?

The possibilities were endless, and every single one made my pussy clench with anticipation.

I dried off quickly and stood naked in front of my bedroom mirror, taking inventory. My body wasn't perfect—I had stretch marks on my hips, my breasts weren't as perky as they'd been in my early twenties, there was a softness to my stomach that no amount of manual labor could entirely eliminate.

But Samson had looked at this body with hunger. Had touched it with reverence and possession in equal measure. Had told me I was beautiful, and for the first time in my life, I'd actually believed it.

I pulled out my best lingerie set—the only nice one I owned, purchased on sale years ago for a special occasion that had never materialized. Black lace, sheer enough to be provocative while still technically covering things. The thong was practically nonexistent, just a whisper of fabric that left almost nothing to the imagination. The bra pushed my breasts up and together, creating cleavage I didn't naturally possess.

I looked at myself in the mirror and felt a surge of confidence. This would drive Samson crazy. I knew it.

For clothing, I chose a short leather skirt I'd bought at a thrift store on impulse and never worn—it had seemed too bold, too sexy, too unlike me. But tonight, it was perfect. It hit mid-thigh and moved beautifully when I walked, the material soft and supple against my skin.

The top was more daring—a cropped thing that revealed my midriff, with thin straps and a neckline that dipped low enough to hint at the lace beneath. Combined with the skirt, the overall effect was sexy without being trashy. Provocative without trying too hard.

I styled my hair in loose waves that cascaded over my shoulders, applied makeup with a heavier hand than usual—smoky eyes, dark lips, a hint of shimmer on my cheekbones. When I was done, I looked like someone confident and sexual and completely in control.

I looked like someone who knew exactly what she wanted.

The transformation should have felt like a costume, like I was playing dress-up again. Instead, it felt like revealing something that had always been there, just waiting for permission to emerge.

I checked the clock: 6:47 PM.

Two hours and thirteen minutes until nine o'clock.

I groaned and collapsed onto my couch, trying to find something—anything—to occupy my mind. The TV went on, some mindless reality show that I couldn't focus on enough to follow. I paced around my small house, reorganizing things that didn't need reorganizing, checking my appearance in every reflective surface.

Despite the cold—the house was freezing as always—I felt uncomfortably warm. My skin was flushed, my body humming with anticipation and nervous energy that had nowhere to go.

I checked the clock again: 6:52 PM.

"This is insane," I muttered to myself. "You're losing your mind."

But I couldn't help it. My hormones and emotions had completely taken over rational thought. I was being led by pure desire, and there was nothing I could do to rein it in.

I tried sitting still. Tried watching TV. Tried reading a book. Nothing worked. The minutes crawled by with agonizing slowness, each one feeling like an hour.

7:15. 7:23. 7:41.

I was going to drive myself crazy at this rate.

Finally—finally—the clock showed 8:30 PM. Close enough.

I grabbed my heels—a different pair from last night, slightly higher and more deliberately sexy—and my purse, then headed out to my car.

The engine struggled when I turned the key, coughing and wheezing in protest. For a terrifying moment, I thought it wasn't going to start, and I had visions of having to call a cab or literally walk to the Den in heels.

But the engine caught on the third try, and I was so relieved and excited that nothing could dampen my mood. If I'd had to walk, I would have done it gladly.

The drive to the Den was surreal. The streets were mostly empty at this hour on a weeknight, streetlights casting orange pools of illumination as I navigated through town.

My hands gripped the steering wheel tightly, my heart already racing even though I was still fifteen minutes away.

I pulled into the parking lot at 8:40—twenty minutes early, but I couldn't stand to wait at home any longer. The Den's building was dark except for a few lights on the upper floors, and the parking lot was empty except for one sleek black Mercedes that I recognized immediately.

Samson's car.

He was here. Waiting for me.

The thought sent a thrill through my entire body.

I killed my engine and sat there for a moment, trying to calm my racing heart. Twenty minutes. I could wait twenty minutes. I pulled out my phone and opened a game app, thinking I could distract myself.

But I kept losing because I couldn't focus on the screen. My mind kept drifting to what was waiting for me inside that building. To Samson and his dark eyes and skilled hands. To finally—finally—feeling him inside me the way I'd been craving.

At 8:58, I couldn't take it anymore.

I got out of my car, smoothed down my skirt, and walked toward the entrance on heels that clicked against the pavement with each step. As I got closer, I noticed something that definitely hadn't been there during my previous visits.

A red carpet had been rolled out from the parking lot to the front doors.

My steps faltered. Had Samson done this? For me?

The gesture was so over-the-top, so romantic and unnecessary and perfect that I felt tears prick at my eyes. I blinked them back furiously—I was not going to ruin my makeup crying before I even made it inside— and continued forward.

The doors were unlocked. I pulled one open and stepped into the lobby.

And stopped in my tracks.

The Den was empty. Completely, utterly empty in a way I'd never seen before. Every other time I'd been here, the place had been buzzing with activity—employees at desks, customers in chairs, the quiet hum of business being conducted.

Now there was nothing. No one. Just silence and dimmed lighting that cast long shadows across the expensive furniture and polished floors.

My heart was pounding so hard I could hear it in my ears, could feel my pulse throbbing in my neck and wrists. All the excitement and anticipation from earlier had transformed into nervous energy. I felt like an innocent schoolgirl about to lose her virginity, anxious and eager and terrified all at once.

Which was ridiculous. I wasn't a virgin. I'd had sex before—admittedly not great sex, but sex nonetheless. This shouldn't feel so monumental.

But it did. It absolutely did.

I worked up my nerve and headed for the employee door that led to the upper floors. My heels echoed in the empty lobby, each step loud and deliberate in the silence.

I pulled the employee door open and immediately noticed something new: a trail of rose petals leading up the stairway.

Red, deep and velvety, creating a path for me to follow. They led up the stairs, down the hallway with its expensive artwork, and ended at Samson's office door.

My breath caught in my throat. My hands were shaking as I reached for the door handle.

This was it. No more anticipation. No more waiting. Whatever was going to happen between Marcus and me, it started the moment I opened this door.

I turned the handle and pushed.

The sight that greeted me made me gasp audibly.

Candles. Dozens of them scattered throughout the office. On the desk, the bookshelves, the mantle of the fireplace, the windowsills. Their flames flickered gently in the still air, casting a warm, golden glow over everything and making shadows dance on the walls.

The rose petal path continued from the doorway across the polished floor to the white rug in the center of the room—the same rug where Samson had made me kneel on that first day, where he'd whipped me and eaten my ass and made me beg.

The memory sent a shiver down my spine, but I wasn't worried about another rough session tonight. The atmosphere Samson had created with the candles and roses was softer, more romantic. This wasn't about dominance and pain.

This was about something else entirely.

I stepped into the office and closed the door behind me with a soft click. The movement stirred the air, and several candle flames swayed wildly, making the shadows on the walls writhe and twist.

I looked around the room, searching for Samson, and found him sitting in a large leather armchair in the far corner—positioned so he had a perfect view of the entire office, including the door I'd just entered through.

He'd been watching me. Watching my reaction to his setup, to the candles and roses and romantic atmosphere he'd created.

Our eyes met across the room, and the intensity in his gaze made my knees weak.

He was dressed more casually than I'd ever seen him—no suit jacket, just dark slacks and a white dress shirt with the sleeves rolled up to his elbows, the top few buttons undone to reveal a hint of his chest. He looked relaxed, but the way he watched me was anything but casual.

He looked like a predator watching his prey walk willingly into his trap.

And God help me, I wanted to be caught.

My feet followed the rose petal path automatically, carrying me to the edge of the white rug. I stopped there, suddenly uncertain. What did he want me to do? Should I speak? Move closer? Wait for instructions?

Samson just stared at me, his eyes traveling slowly down the length of my body—lingering on my legs in the short skirt, the exposed skin of my midriff, the swell of my breasts visible above my low neckline. The heat in his gaze was palpable, and I felt it like a physical touch.

I slipped my feet out of my heels, needing to feel grounded, and pushed them aside with my toes. The rug was soft beneath my bare feet, familiar from that first day.

I waited for Samson to say something, to give me direction, but he remained silent. Just watching. Waiting.

Fine. If he wasn't going to make the first move, I would.

I walked slowly toward him, my hips swaying with each step, putting a little extra movement into it because I could see the way his eyes tracked my approach with laser focus. When I reached the chair, I leaned down and pressed my lips to his.

For a moment, Samson remained still, letting me take the lead. Then his mouth parted, his tongue grazing along my lips in a gentle request for entry that sent electricity down my spine.

I gasped against his mouth, and my back arched involuntarily as another shiver coursed through me. My pussy was already wet, already aching for him, and we'd barely touched.

I climbed onto the chair without breaking the kiss, straddling his lap with my knees on either side of his hips. My hands cupped his face, fingers threading into his hair as I pulled him closer, deepening the kiss.

Samson's hands came to rest on my back, warm and strong as they caressed from my shoulders downward in long, soothing strokes. It was tender, almost reverent—so different from the dominance he'd shown before.

His hands reached the hem of my skirt and slipped beneath it, pushing the leather up around my waist. Then his palms were on my ass, cupping and squeezing.

I moaned against his mouth and reached down between us to rub his cock through his pants. He was already hard—I could feel the thick length of him straining against the fabric, hot and ready.

My fingers fumbled with his zipper for a moment before managing to pull it down. Then I was reaching into his pants, my hand wrapping around his bare shaft, and the feel of him in my palm made me whimper with need.

God, he felt good. Hot and thick and perfect.

One of Samson's fingers slid under the edge of my thong, tracing along the curve of my ass. The touch was light, almost ticklish, but it sent sparks of pleasure through me. His finger traveled lower, following the crack between my cheeks, until it reached my pussy.

He rubbed between my labia with gentle pressure, and I felt my arousal increase tenfold, coating his finger with wetness.

I pumped his shaft slowly, keeping a firm grip, savoring the weight and heat of him in my hand. All the foreplay we'd engaged in over the past few days had been incredible—better than anything I'd experienced before. But tonight felt different. Tonight, the foreplay was just a formality, a precursor to what we both really wanted.

His finger pressed inside my pussy, sliding into me with ease, and I gasped at the intrusion. My hand tightened around his cock involuntarily, my legs twitching as pleasure shot through me.

Samson broke away from my lips and began kissing his way down my neck in a trail of heat and sensation. His teeth nibbled gently on my flesh—not hard enough to hurt, just enough to send warmth cascading through my body.

I tilted my head to the side, giving him better access, and he took advantage by sucking on my collarbone while his finger continued to slide in and out of my pussy.

"Oh God," I groaned, clenching my walls around his finger, trying to hold him inside. "Please. Take me. I need you to take me."

The words tumbled out before I could stop them, raw and desperate.

"Please, daddy," I heard myself whisper. "I need you inside me."

The pet name slipped out without conscious thought, but it felt right. Samson had positioned himself as the authority figure in our arrangement, the one in control, the one who decided when and how and what. Calling him daddy was just acknowledging that dynamic out loud.

And from the way his breath hitched and his cock pulsed in my hand, he liked it.

A lot.

CHAPTER 18

Samson's response to my plea was immediate and visceral.

His teeth clamped down harder on my collarbone—not quite painful, but firm enough to send a jolt through my system—and I felt a second finger press into my pussy alongside the first.

The stretch was intense, my inner walls struggling to accommodate the added girth, and a sound somewhere between a whimper and a moan escaped my throat. I felt full in a way I hadn't with just one finger, and the pressure was exquisite.

"That's it," Samson murmured against my skin. "Take it, baby. Take what I give you."

I started working my hips, grinding down on his fingers, forcing them deeper while my hand continued pumping his cock. My other hand fumbled with his belt, fingers clumsy with need, trying to free him completely.

I couldn't stand it anymore. Couldn't wait another second. I needed his cock inside me, needed to feel him stretching me, filling me, claiming me in every way possible.

Samson must have sensed my desperation—or maybe he shared it—because suddenly he was moving, scooting forward in the chair. The shift in position made me feel like I was going to fall backward, and I gasped in alarm.

But Samson's arms wrapped around me, holding me tightly against his chest as he slid off the edge of the chair with controlled grace. We landed on the rug with him on top of me, his hands braced on either side of my head to keep from crushing me with his weight.

For a moment, we just stared at each other, our faces inches apart, both breathing hard. His pupils were blown wide with desire, his hair mussed from my fingers, and he'd never looked more devastating.

I reached up and started unbuttoning his shirt with frantic fingers, pulling at the material with such enthusiasm that several buttons popped off and skittered across the floor. I didn't care. I just needed the barrier gone, needed to feel his skin against mine.

The shirt came off—or at least was pushed out of the way—and I leaned up to shower his chest with kisses. His skin was warm and firm beneath my lips, and I could feel his heart pounding just as hard as mine.

Our hands were everywhere at once, pulling at clothes, caressing heated skin, desperate for more contact. Samson's fingers found the hem of my top and yanked it over my head, then made quick work of my bra clasp with the kind of expertise that would have made me jealous if I could focus on anything beyond the way his hands felt on my bare breasts.

"God, you're perfect," he breathed, his thumbs brushing over my nipples. "So fucking perfect."

I managed to work his pants down to his thighs, and his cock finally sprang free—thick and hard and ready. I wrapped my hand around him immediately, stroking with an intensity born of pent-up desire.

Samson groaned and kicked his pants off the rest of the way, then positioned himself between my spread legs. My skirt had ridden up around my waist, and he hooked his fingers into my thong and pulled it aside rather than taking the time to remove it completely.

His crown pressed against my entrance, and every muscle in my body tensed in anticipation.

This was it. Finally, finally it was happening.

"Look at me," Samson commanded, and my eyes snapped to his. "I want to see your face when I make you mine."

Then he was pushing inside, and the feeling was so intense I forgot how to breathe.

There was pressure at the entrance of my pussy as my body stretched to accommodate his size, and then he was sliding deeper, his entire shaft filling me in one slow, relentless thrust.

"Fuck!" I moaned, my nails raking down his back hard enough to probably leave marks. My legs trembled on either side of his hips, my body caught between the instinct to pull him closer and the overwhelming sensation of being so completely filled.

But then he paused, giving me time to adjust, and began moving his hips in slow, shallow thrusts that gradually eased the tightness.

"You're so tight," he whispered against my ear, his hot breath sending shivers down my spine. "So perfect. Taking me so well."

His right hand slid down my side and under my bunched-up skirt, his thumb finding my clit with unerring accuracy. He began rubbing circles around the sensitive bundle of nerves while continuing those slow, deep thrusts.

The dual stimulation was overwhelming. I could feel an orgasm building already, the tingling sensation starting deep and spreading outward like wildfire. My legs began to convulse, trembling uncontrollably as pleasure mounted with terrifying speed.

My entire body went numb for a few seconds, every sensation intensifying to the point where I thought I might actually black out. Colors burst behind my closed eyelids. My pussy clamped down on Samson's cock. Sound became muffled, distant, like I was underwater.

I'd never come this hard, this fast, this completely before.

Marcus stopped moving, his expression shifting from pleasure to concern. "Madison? What's wrong?"

"Nothing," I managed to gasp, though my voice sounded strange to my own ears. "Just... give me a second."

My pussy was still throbbing, aftershocks pulsing through me in waves. My clit was so sensitive that even the brush of his thumb against it was almost unbearable. Samson did his best not to move, but the fact that his cock was still buried deep inside me meant every tiny shift sent sparks of oversensitized pleasure through my system.

My walls shuddered around him, and I closed my eyes, waiting for the intensity to dissipate enough that I could function again.

It took longer than I expected—probably a full minute, though it felt like an eternity. But finally, finally, the overwhelming sensitivity began to fade to something manageable.

I pushed against Samson's chest, and he pulled out immediately, giving me space. I rolled onto my stomach, getting onto my hands and knees, then lifted my ass up in invitation and looked at him over my shoulder.

"Fuck me," I said, licking my lips deliberately. "I want you to really fuck me this time."

Something dark and hungry flashed in Samson's eyes. He moved behind me, gripping his cock and angling it back into my pussy. Then he began thrusting with a passion and ferocity that made that first slow claiming seem tame by comparison.

His hips slammed against my ass with enough force that my arms almost buckled. The sound of skin slapping against skin filled the office, punctuated by my screams of pleasure that I couldn't have suppressed if I tried.

I was so wet that my arousal was dripping down my mound, creating obscene wet sounds with each thrust. The rug beneath my knees was probably getting ruined, but I couldn't bring myself to care about anything beyond the feeling of Samson pounding into me.

My knees were starting to get sore from the sustained pressure, but I pushed through the discomfort. I didn't want to stop—

wouldn't stop—until Samson was finished, until he'd taken everything he wanted from my willing body.

His hands grabbed my shoulders, fingers digging into my flesh as he pulled me back to meet each forward thrust of his hips. The angle drove him impossibly deeper, his crown brushing against my cervix with each stroke.

"Oh, yes!" I cried out, past caring who might hear, past caring about anything except this moment. "Yes, yes, just like that!"

Samson's cock plunged in and out of my hole with forceful rhythm, sending vibrations through me that made my clit ache with renewed need. I could feel another orgasm building, slower this time but somehow even more intense.

Then Samson's hand moved into my hair, his fingers tangling in the strands before pulling hard enough to jerk my head back. My spine arched at the forced angle, and he kept pulling until I was upright on my knees, my hands reaching back to grip his legs for balance.

His other hand came around to my throat—not choking, just resting there with light pressure that made me feel claimed, possessed. His hand slid upward to my mouth, and I sucked his fingers without being asked, tasting salt and skin and my own arousal.

I reached between my legs with one hand and found his balls, massaging them gently while he continued pounding into my pussy from behind. I wanted to feel him come. Needed to know I could make him lose control the way he'd made me lose it.

"Fill me," I groaned around his finger, my voice muffled but desperate. "Please, daddy. Fill my pussy with your cum."

Samson grunted—a deep, rumbling sound I could feel reverberating in his chest where it pressed against my back. His thrusts became more erratic, losing their steady rhythm as his own orgasm approached.

"Fuck," he growled. "Madison, I'm going to—"

"Do it," I demanded. "Come inside me. I want to feel it."

With one final, powerful thrust that drove the breath from my lungs, Samson buried himself as deep as he could go. I felt his cock pulse and then erupt, hot cum shooting from his crown.

"Holy shit," he moaned, and the raw pleasure in his voice sent me over the edge again.

My second orgasm was different from the first—less explosive, more rolling, like waves crashing against a shore. My pussy clenched rhythmically around Samson's still-spurting cock, milking him for every drop.

He released my hair and throat, and I fell forward onto my hands with a loud thump that probably echoed through the empty building. I pushed my ass back against him and deliberately clenched my walls, trying to hold him inside as long as possible.

Samson's cock pulsed a few more times, more of his release coating my insides, marking me from within. Finally, when we were both spent and trembling, I slowly pulled forward, feeling his softening cock slip from my body.

I crawled the short distance to the center of the rug and rolled onto my back, staring up at the ceiling where candlelight created dancing shadows. My chest heaved with exertion, my heart drumming so hard against my ribs I could feel it in my throat.

Samson followed me, lying down beside me and placing his left hand on my thigh. The touch was gentle, almost tender—such a contrast to the way he'd just fucked me.

I put my hand on top of his and laced our fingers together, and for a long moment, we just lay there in silence, catching our breath and processing what had just happened.

The weight of reality was starting to settle over me like a heavy blanket.

This was the final day of our contract. Three days, as promised. Marcus would fulfill his end of the bargain—he'd forgive Grandma's debt, save her house, and in return I'd given him my body three times in whatever way he wanted.

The arrangement was complete. Our deal was over.

The thought made my chest ache with a pain that had nothing to do with physical exertion.

I didn't want this to be over. Didn't want to go back to my life before Samson—the cold apartment, the soul-crushing job, the endless struggle to make ends meet. And more than that, I didn't want to lose him. Didn't want to never see him again, never feel his hands on my skin, never hear him call me a good girl in that voice that made my knees weak.

Life would be empty without Samson in it. The realization hit me with the force of a physical blow.

I rolled onto my side to look at him, and he turned his head to meet my gaze. His hair was mussed, his lips swollen from kissing, his eyes still dark with residual desire. He'd never looked more beautiful.

"My grandmother's debt is forgiven?" I asked quietly, needing to hear him confirm it one more time.

"Yes," Samson answered without hesitation. "The debt is completely forgiven. The paperwork will be processed tomorrow, and your grandmother will receive official notification within the week. Her house is safe."

"Thank you," I whispered, and felt tears beginning to sting my eyes as the full weight of what I was about to lose crashed over me.

Samson noticed immediately. His free hand came up to cup my cheek, his thumb gently wiping away a tear that had escaped and was trailing down toward my temple.

"What's wrong?" he asked, concern etched into his features. "Did I hurt you? Was I too rough?"

"No, it's not that. It's..." I took a shaky breath, trying to find the courage to say what I was feeling.

Should I tell him? Should I expose my heart like this, risk the humiliation of having my feelings dismissed or, worse, pitied?

But what did I have to lose? The arrangement was over anyway. In a few minutes, I'd get dressed and leave this office and probably never see him again except as a distant figure in town—the powerful bank president who'd once done me a favor.

I might as well be honest.

"I think I'm in love with you," I confessed, the words tumbling out in a rush before I could stop them.

The moment they were out, I wanted to take them back. Wanted to laugh and say I was joking, that it was just post-orgasm endorphins talking, that I didn't mean it.

But I did mean it. God help me, I meant every word.

Samson went very still beside me, his expression impossible to read. The silence stretched between us, growing heavier with each passing second, and I felt my heart begin to crack.

This was it. This was where he'd gently let me down, thank me for my services, and send me on my way with my dignity in tatters.

I started to pull away, to save us both the awkwardness of him having to reject me, but Samson's hand tightened on mine, holding me in place.

"Say that again," he said quietly.

I swallowed hard. "I think... I think I'm in love with you."

"You think?" A small smile tugged at the corner of his mouth. "Or you know?"

"I—" I stopped, considered. Was I just confused? Mixing up great sex with actual feelings? Mistaking gratitude and power dynamics for love?

No. This was real. I knew it with a certainty I'd never felt about anything before.

"I know," I said firmly. "I love you."

Samson's smile widened, and he rolled to face me fully, his body pressing against mine along its entire length.

"Good," he said simply. "Because I'm in love with you too."

The words didn't register at first. I stared at him, certain I'd misheard, that my desperate brain had manufactured the response I wanted to hear.

"What?"

"I love you, Madison Carter." He said it slowly, deliberately, like he wanted to make absolutely sure I understood. "I've been falling for you since the moment you stormed into my office ready to fight me for your grandmother's house. Maybe even before that, if I'm being honest."

"But... the contract. The arrangement. This was supposed to be just—"

"Business?" Samson finished. "Yes, that's how it started. But somewhere between that first day and tonight, it became something else entirely. At least for me."

Tears were flowing freely now, but for an entirely different reason. "Then why didn't you say anything? Why let me think—"

"Because I wanted you to have the choice," Samson interrupted gently. "Our arrangement had a power imbalance from the start. I was holding your grandmother's security over your head, whether intentionally or not. I needed to know that if you felt something for me, it was real—not just gratitude or obligation or Stockholm syndrome."

He brushed his thumb across my cheek again, catching another tear.

"So I waited," he continued. "I waited for our contract to be fulfilled, for the debt to be paid, for you to be free of any obligation to me. And then I was going to ask—properly ask, not command—if you'd be willing to see me again. To give us a chance at something real."

"You were?" I could barely get the words out around the lump in my throat.

"I was. I am." Samson leaned forward and kissed me softly, tenderly, in a way that had nothing to do with sex and everything to do with the words we'd just exchanged.

"Madison, I know the circumstances of how we got here are complicated. I know there's a significant age difference, and that I'm your mother's ex-husband, and that society will have opinions about all of it. But I don't care about any of that if you don't."

"I don't," I said immediately. "I don't care what anyone thinks."

"Then here's what I'm proposing," Samson said, his tone shifting into something more businesslike—but his eyes remained warm, full of emotion. "No more contracts. No more arrangements. Just us, seeing where this goes naturally. I'd like to take you on actual dates. Court you properly. Get to know all the parts of you that aren't related to our original agreement."

"Court me?" I couldn't help but smile at the old-fashioned phrasing.

"Yes. Court you. Wine and dine you. Take you places, show you things, treat you the way you deserve to be treated." His expression grew more serious. "And Madison? I want to help you. Not because of any obligation or arrangement, but because I care about you and I have the resources to make your life easier. Let me fix your heat. Your water heater. Your car. Let me help you find a job that doesn't make you miserable. You don't have to struggle anymore if you don't want to."

He knew about the problems with my house? Of course he did. He seemed to know everything. And the offer was tempting—so tempting it made my chest ache. But I had to be honest.

"I don't want to be bought," I said quietly. "I don't want to be another thing you own."

"You could never be that," Marcus said firmly. "You're not something to be owned, Madison. You're someone to be cherished. Someone to be partnered with. And if accepting my help makes you uncomfortable, we'll work out a different arrangement—you can pay me back over time, or we can call it a loan, or whatever makes you feel better about it. But please, let me help you. Let me take care of you the way I want to."

I studied his face, looking for any sign of manipulation or ulterior motive. But all I saw was sincerity and hope and love.

Love.

Samson Lang loved me.

The thought was still almost impossible to believe, but the evidence was right there in his eyes.

"Okay," I whispered. "Yes. To all of it. Dates and courting and help and whatever else you want to offer. Yes."

His smile was brilliant, transforming his entire face. "Yeah?"

"Yeah." I laughed, giddy with sudden joy. "God, yes."

Samson kissed me again, deeper this time, and I wrapped my arms around his neck and poured everything I was feeling into the kiss. Relief and happiness and love and desire all tangled together into something so intense it made me dizzy.

When we finally broke apart, both breathing hard again, Samson rested his forehead against mine.

"Stay with me tonight," he murmured. "Come home with me. Let me wake up with you in my bed."

"I'd like that," I said. "I'd like that very much."

We lay there for a while longer, wrapped in each other's arms on that expensive rug surrounded by flickering candles, and for the first time in as long as I could remember, I felt genuinely, completely happy.

The contract was over.

But we were just beginning.

THE END

About the Author

Genevieve Kinsman has always been fascinated by the space between want and need, power and surrender. Her stories explore the delicious tension of forbidden desire, featuring alpha heroes who know what they want and heroines strong enough to make them work for it.

A former corporate manager who left for dirty talk, Genevieve now spends her days crafting romance novels that explore age gaps, morally complex characters, and relationships that develop in the most unlikely circumstances.

When she's not writing, you'll find her sipping wine that costs more than it should, collecting vintage romance novels, and defending the artistic merit of spicy romance to anyone who'll listen.

She currently resides in a city she won't name with a partner who's learned not to ask what she's researching.